D1366290

B

OKLAHOMA WEDDINGS, BOOK 3

By His Hand

HARDWORKING MAN MEETS SOFTHEARTED WOMAN IN THIS CONTEMPORARY NOVEL

JENNIFER JOHNSON

THORNDIKE PRESS
A part of Gale, Cengage Learning

GALE
CENGAGE Learning

Detroit • New York • San Francisco • New Haven, Conn • Waterville, Maine • London

GALE
CENGAGE Learning⁻

Thorndike Press® Large Print Christian Fiction.
The text of this Large Print edition is unabridged.
Other aspects of the book may vary from the original edition.
Set in 16 pt. Plantin.
Printed on permanent paper.

LIBRARY OF CONGRESS CATALOGING-IN-PUBLICATION DATA

Johnson, Jennifer.
    By his hand / by Jennifer Johnson.
      p. cm. — (Thorndike Press large print Christian fiction)
    "Hardworking man meets softhearted woman in this
contemporary novel [from] Oklahoma weddings, book three."
    ISBN-13: 978-1-4104-0997-3 (hardcover : alk. paper)
    ISBN-10: 1-4104-0997-X (hardcover : alk. paper)
      1. Oklahoma—Fiction. 2. Large type books. I. Oklahoma
weddings. II. Title.
PS3610.O356B9 2008
813'.6—dc22   2008021516

Published in 2008 by arrangement with Barbour Publishing, Inc.

Printed in the United States of America
1 2 3 4 5 6 7 12 11 10 09 08

DEDICATION

This story is dedicated to my husband, Albert.

You've been my Prince Charming for nearly two decades.

My heart still pitter-patters when I see you.

I still care about what you think and feel. I still want your very best.

After all this time, you still hang the moon.

Through thick and thin, we've learned what love truly is —

a First Corinthians 13 kind of love. Wow, how I praise God for you.

With that said, how could I keep from thanking and praising my Abba?

Praise You, Jesus. Your mercies never end, and they never fail. I love you.

Prologue

There is a time for everything, and a
season for every activity under heaven.
ECCLESIASTES 3:1

Disinfectant couldn't mask the stench of
iodine mingled with other unidentifiable
odors. The mixture stung Victoria Thankful's nostrils and brought tears to her eyes.
She looked at the hospital bed. She had
never seen anyone like this, but this was her
brother.

Kenny's practically lifeless body lay still.
Stitches raced from the left side of his
forehead over his nose and finished at the
right corner of his lips. Both eyes were black
and swollen from the impact to the windshield.

"Hey, Bubby," she crooned his pet name
since childhood and patted his arm. "I'm
waiting for you to open those eyes and look
at me."

Heavily drugged, Kenny had only spoken a few times over the last three days. He needed rest, but the doctors still wanted him to talk to her every few hours in an effort to keep up his spirits.

"I sent Grams home. She was needing a shower." She swatted her hand before her nose and laughed at her own joke, hoping it would conjure a smile from her brother.

He didn't move. *I'm sure he's sleeping.* She glanced at her watch. It had been two hours since he'd spoken to her. In that time, she'd swallowed down a day-old deli sandwich and finished an Algebra II test one of her friends had brought by the hospital.

A nurse opened the door. "Your parents are on the way."

"Thank you." Victoria sighed in relief and looked back at Kenny. "Mother and Daddy have come back from Europe early. I know they're anxious to see that you're all right."

Victoria glanced down at her clothes. Her mother would disapprove of the sweatshirt and jeans. She walked to the sink and peeked in the mirror. *She's not going to like my hair all pulled back in a ponytail either.*

Walking back to her brother, she wasn't worried about outfits and hairstyles. She only cared about Kenny and seeing him healed and healthy.

"Sis?" His weak voice pushed past barely open lips. He opened his eyes slowly and turned his palm up, inviting her to grab his hand.

Bubble gum stuck to the roof of her mouth. The raspy weakness of his voice still struck her hard. Pushing her hand past tubes and wires, she tried to ignore the machines' protesting beeps at having been jostled. She forced a smile.

"Do we know" — he swallowed — "how bad it is?"

"Let's not worry." She winked and sat in the chair beside his bed. "It's going to be okay."

It wasn't okay. She knew medicine and doctors could fix a ton of ailments and injuries, and she believed anything was possible with God. Still, it didn't appear it was going to be all right at all.

"So tired." Kenny closed his eyes.

She squeezed his hand. "I'm here for you, Kenny. We'll get through." Fear lurked around her, waiting for her to succumb to it. *Give me strength, Lord.*

"Doctor," her father's voice boomed from outside the door. "I'll pay whatever it takes. You make him perfect."

"Your son is in guarded condition. We are doing the best we can. His accident was serious."

Victoria jumped up. *There's no telling what Daddy will say.* She wiggled her hand past the tubes and wires then made a beeline for the door.

"I'm sure you know the Thankful name," her father continued. "I want only the best — everyone, everything. No cost spared. Make him perfect."

"Money isn't the answer to everything. This is a back injury. No amount of money . . ."

"It would have been better if he had died," her mother whispered.

Victoria forced the door shut. She looked at her brother. His eyes were closed, and she prayed he hadn't heard her mother's response. Victoria made her way back to him. She touched his leg and remembered he couldn't feel it. She walked back to the top of the bed, leaned over, and kissed the top of his head. "You're going to be all right."

CHAPTER 1

Eight Years Later

After twelve hours of chugging java to stay awake, Victoria finally spotted the specific road sign she'd been looking for. She gasped. "Forty more miles on this road! I'm never going to get to Lasso, Oklahoma."

Resting against the leather seat of her Suburban, she glanced at the photograph taped to her dashboard. The boy's shining eyes and chubby cheeks made her smile. "You look so much like your daddy." She ran her finger over his brown ringlets, remembering the last time she'd seen her brother before his fatal accident. His hair had been in desperate need of a trim, and Victoria had teased him mercilessly about it. "Kenny would have been so proud of you, Matthew."

At midmorning, the flat, green land stretched as far as she could see. An occasional farmhouse, barn, or silo dotted the expanse. Cattle clustered inside the never-ending barbed wire. *I'm definitely not in Houston anymore.* Oklahoma was full and alive in a different way, and its serenity beckoned her.

She yawned and started to roll down the window to allow wisps of fresh air to wake her up. Bubble gum and fast-food wrappers swirled through the cab. Grabbing for her directions and the photograph, she popped the window back up. *What was I thinking?*

She pushed the disheveled papers off the passenger seat and laid the directions in their place. *No way am I getting lost. I'll fall asleep for sure if I have to drive one moment longer than necessary.*

Course, I'd fit just fine if I needed to take a nap in this horse of a car. Daddy would never see to reason on allowing her to get a smaller, more economical car. Ever since Kenny's accidents, one paralyzing him and the other taking his life, Daddy had bought only the biggest and best of every model. "He never considered what gas would cost, though, did he?"

She gripped the steering wheel. *I don't even have the means to get back to Texas if I need to.* She cringed when she thought of the penthouse, finely decorated in the sleek-est of styles, that she'd left behind. It had

12

been Daddy's idea to fit her in the best of everything while she finished her degree. She couldn't afford any of it now.

God has not equipped me with a spirit of fear. She lifted her chin. She would not be afraid. Money was not the answer to everything. God was.

She braked at a stoplight. She smiled as she read the wooden road sign aloud. "Welcome to Lawton."

"One more turn, then sixty miles to the small town of Lasso . . . and to Matthew." She opened her visor mirror. "Ugh. These freckles." She hated them. They made her look much younger than her age. She grabbed her compact from her Gucci bag and powdered her nose and cheeks. "There."

She turned on the radio, hoping she could pick up a Christian radio signal out here in the middle of nowhere. "Yep. That's where I'm at." She patted her steering wheel. "My whole life is in the middle of nowhere." She looked up at the boundless, blue sky above her. "I'm a clean slate, Lord. Whatever You want. Wherever You wish." The reality of it made her smile . . . and tremble.

"That little sister of mine is determined to put me six feet under," growled Chris Rat-

13

liff as he finished buffing the candy-apple red hood of his pride and joy, a restored 1973 Corvette. After grabbing a clean, white cloth from his back coveralls pocket, he wiped off the rearview mirror. "You, my Mary Ann, will never make me crazy."

As a boy, he and his dad spent many an afternoon watching reruns of *Gilligan's Island.* Both agreed Mary Ann to be their favorite character. She had been the true beauty with her natural good looks and sweet, giving nature. When his dad gave him the beat-up car for a graduation present eight years ago, he knew she could be named nothing but Mary Ann.

"I said I was sorry. Promise, I didn't mean to."

Chris glared at his sister, Abby. She shoved both hands in her jeans pockets. The plaid button-down shirt she wore hung much too big on her — which made sense. It belonged to him. With her mousy brown hair pulled up in some sort of funky knot with pieces sticking out around her head, she looked like she'd stuck her finger in a light socket. For the life of him, he wasn't sure if she meant to look that way or if she just didn't have a clue about how to brush hair. He didn't know the first thing about it.

Seventeen, hardheaded, difficult, and an overall nuisance, Abby was his to raise. Even after she'd slammed into the mailbox with his work truck, he still loved her and wouldn't want her anywhere else except with him.

Well, maybe not at the moment. "Abby, you get back in that house."

"Brudder." She stuck out her bottom lip.

Oh, brother. Abby always pulled out her childhood name for him when she knew she was in trouble. Admittedly it usually worked. This time he needed to be firm. "You know you didn't have permission to drive it. Go on back in there until I decide your punishment."

"Fine, Chris." She spat out his name, emphasizing the *s*. "Just remember I was goin' to the store to get some milk for breakfast." She strode back to the house and slammed the door.

Chris knew he should go after her and make her apologize, but it was hard. Growing up, he and his sister bickered back and forth. Mom and Dad had been the ones to separate, scold, or paddle them for misbehavior. Less than two years had passed since their dad had died and only a year since their mom left. *I don't know how to be her guardian, Lord. I'm her brother.*

He sulked to the garden, grabbed a bucket from beside the scarecrow, and picked tomatoes from the vine. Most of them were still green; nothing had ripened for picking, but he had to do something. Had to think.

No, he needed advice. He needed to talk to someone who would know what to do. Someone he could trust. He smacked his thigh. *I know. I'll run out to the Wards' ranch.* Snapping off a few more tomatoes, he threw them in the bucket figuring Sondra could make fried green tomatoes or whatnot with them.

He walked back to the house and stepped inside the mudroom. Grabbing his keys off the counter, he hollered, "Abby, I'll be right back. You get lunch going and don't leave this house."

"Fine!"

Fury pulsed through his veins. He shouldn't let her talk to him like that. *If I say something now, I'm sure I'll regret it later.*

He stalked to his car, jumped into Mary Ann's driver's seat, and revved the engine. The growling *purr* sent a calm through this veins. *Now here's a girl a guy can relate to.* He pulled out of the driveway and headed to Dylan and Sondra's ranch.

Extra cautious with his prized treasure, he stopped at the first intersection as the light turned yellow. *I just can't seem to do it, Lord. I don't know what to do with Abby.* Flipping the radio on, one of his favorite country gospel songs sounded from the speakers. The words of God's faithfulness were a soothing balm to the anger and frustration lit in his heart, reminding him he was not alone. *Thank You, Lord.*

Mentally he processed the chords and notes playing from the guitar. This song was perfect for his church's worship team. He'd already ordered the sheet music and could hardly wait until it arrived at Lawton's Christian Bookstore.

He glanced in his rearview mirror. A Suburban bounded toward him. His heart began to pound. "No!" He gripped the steering wheel. "Please, oh, please, no!"

Metal crunched against metal.

CHAPTER 2

Victoria pushed the air bag away from her chest and face. Fanning the dust particles away with one hand, she coughed and opened the door. She scampered out and looked at the smaller car in front of her.

Please, God, don't let the driver be hurt. Memories of Kenny's beaten body lying in the hospital bed replayed in her mind. She froze. *Please, God, make the driver come out.*

Nothing.

She inched closer to the little car. Her heart pounded. *Move, Victoria. The person may need help.* Tears welled in her eyes. She'd nearly passed out when she'd seen Kenny the first time. She couldn't handle blood. She hated pain.

The door flew open, and a man stepped out with no apparent injury. *Thank You, Jesus.* She let out her breath and swiped at her eyes with the back of her hands.

"No!" The man blazed past her and stared

at the back of his car.

"Oh, my." She cupped her hands across her mouth. The impact had broken off the bumper and smashed the whole rear end of the little red Corvette. She didn't know much about cars, but she knew Corvettes were a good kind. Her daddy had one, once upon a time, and Thomas Thankful owned only the best of everything.

She looked at the front of her Suburban. The silver-rack-thingy had dented a bit, but that was the extent of her damage.

"I'm sorry, sir." She peeked down at the overgrown, spitting image of the blond guy from *The Dukes of Hazzard.* Only this man's hair had a red tint to it. He even dressed the part with his mechanic getup covered in grease stains. She wrung her hands together. "I'm glad you're all right. I can't believe I was so careless."

The man stood to his full height, and she nearly swallowed her gum. He towered over her like a daddy to his toddler. Pointing to his chest, he growled, "I'm fine." His jaw set, and he looked anything but willing to accept her apology. He pointed to the Corvette. "Look at my car."

Victoria coughed back the need to duck her head, hide under the asphalt, and enjoy a good cry. She straightened her shoulders.

The fault belonged to her, but she didn't need to fall apart. "I'm sorry."

He glowered at her, his eyes big as silver dollars. Disdain covered his face as he scanned her up and down.

Victoria's confident stance faltered. She shifted her weight from one foot to the other. "My insurance will cover it, I'm sure."

By now a crowd had formed. Heat rose up her back. *Stay calm.* Once her embarrassment reached her shoulder blades, it was all over; her neck and cheeks would be a blotchy mess.

"Mary Ann," the man whispered.

"I didn't hear you, sir." She leaned closer to him; then she noticed one of the men on the sidewalk pointed at her and the car as he whispered into a young girl's ear. Two women stood to the left of them whispering at each other and shaking their heads.

The driver walked away and stood, shoulders slumped, next to the other side of the Corvette. He shoved both hands into his coverall pockets, and she took a few steps toward him. He knelt and picked the bumper off the ground. "Mary Ann."

"Sir, my name is not Mary Ann."

He glared at Victoria as if she'd grown an extra pair of eyeballs, a nose, and an additional head. "Mary Ann is my car." The words spat from his lips much like Daddy's elaborate sprinkler system shot water all over their plush lawn at midmorning and early evening.

"Oh." She stared at her hands. She'd heard of men naming their cars but never understood the notion. "I *am* sorry."

"Do you have any idea how many years I've worked on this car?"

His words were a whisper. Surprisingly, they didn't hold anger. It was pain, and she felt them with more force than a slap to the face. Her heart beat faster. *Help me, Lord. What do I do? What do I say?*

People chattered around her. She could hear them asking who she was and where she was from. "I'm sorry." She couldn't look at the man. The tone in his voice, the slump of his shoulders, everything about him made her feel as though she'd committed a terrible crime. "I know my insurance will pay. . . ."

The screeching of a siren drowned her out. The car stopped, and a sheriff stepped out. "What's goin' on here?" The man hefted his gun belt higher onto his waist.

"She hit Mary Ann."

"I can see that." The sheriff scraped his jaw and shook his head. "She was lookin' mighty good, too."

21

"I've been standing here trying to convince myself she was just a car."

"And I'm sure the lady didn't aim to hit ya."

The driver shook his head and exhaled a long breath. "All that work."

That was it. She couldn't handle any more. *The Dukes of Hazzard* fellow looked as if he planned to give the eulogy at his mother's funeral. It was a car. It was an accident. There had been no injuries. Her insurance would, without a doubt, pay for the repairs.

"Mister, Sheriff, I'm truly sorry. Can we please hurry on with the report?" She glanced at the still-whispering crowd. "I'd like to get to my sister-in-law's house before lunch."

The sheriff pushed back his hat. "Oh sure. I just need your license, registration, and proof of insurance." He addressed the other man. "Yours, too, Chris."

She walked back to her Suburban, leaned through the passenger window, and popped open the glove compartment. She dug through paper after paper looking for her registration and proof of insurance. "Where are they?" She grabbed the whole pile and laid it on the passenger's seat. Going through one piece at a time, Victoria felt heat rising up her back once again.

"Having a bit of trouble?"

The sheriff stepped next to her. Her shoulder blades burned, and her stomach turned. "I'm just trying to find . . . Here it is." She picked up the registration and handed it to him.

"Yep." The sheriff grinned. He already held the man's papers in his hands. "Now all I need is your license and insurance."

"I know." Victoria shuffled through manuals, maintenance lists, and other papers. The murmurs of what had to be the entire town made her hands shake. Placing the last piece of paper in the glove compartment, she exhaled and smacked the side of her hip. "I can't find my insurance."

The sheriff smiled. "Don't worry 'bout it. Just give me your license. I will have to cite you for no insurance, but just as soon as you provide proof to the judge, everything'll be fine."

"Judge?" The vein in Victoria's right temple throbbed.

"Just a formality. Don't worry 'bout it one bit."

Victoria opened the passenger's door. "Do you mind if I sit down a minute?"

"Course not."

She climbed inside then closed her eyes

and leaned back in the seat. What did a real judge look like? The only ones she'd ever seen were the ones on television, and they were often angry and exasperated with the people before them.

Just don't think about that right now. All she had to do was sit a few moments and wait for the sheriff to fix up the paperwork. The leather rested cool against her neck, easing her discomfort a bit.

"I still need your license, ma'am."

Victoria sat up. "I'm sorry." She scooped her purse off the floorboard and rummaged through it. "It's right here in my wallet." She pulled the fuchsia accessory from her bag and snapped it open. Her ID wasn't where it should have been.

"Oh no." Dread filled her as she remembered not being able to find it when the grocery store's cashier asked for it a few weeks before. She thumbed through each card, willing, praying for the card to reveal itself.

"What's the matter?"

The driver had obviously grown tired of waiting. Victoria begged to be awakened from this nightmare as she went through each card in her wallet.

"She can't find her license," the sheriff responded, "or proof of insurance."

Giving in, she leaned back against the seat. "I lost it a couple of weeks ago."

"Then why were you looking for it?" The sheriff folded his arms in front of his chest. His expression transformed to one not so forgiving.

"I — I just hoped maybe I had overlooked it."

"I'm sorry, ma'am. You're driving without a license or proof of insurance. You've caused a wreck." He shook his head. "I'm going to have to take you down to the jail until I can figure out your identity."

"No! Please, my name is Victoria Allison Thankful. I'll tell you anything you want to know. I've lived in . . ."

"You any relation to Sondra Ward? Her name used to be Thankful."

"Yes, yes. She used to be my sister-in-law. I'm here to visit."

"Well, now" — the sheriff smacked his lips together and winked — "we can just give her a call, verify that you're who you say you are, and we'll get you on your way."

"Thank you."

"I hate to do it, but I'll still have to cite you and impound your vehicle."

"What? But how will I get to Sondra's farm?"

"How will I get Mary Ann fixed?"

She glared at the man the sheriff had called Chris. How could he think about that car at this moment? Her life had already collapsed into pieces; now the pieces were shattering.

She dug the cell phone from her jeans pocket and grabbed the stationery from the seat. Dialing Sondra's number, all she could think of was getting away from the crowd and this man. The phone rang. It rang again. *Please pick up. Lord, please let Sondra be there.*

"Hello." Sondra's voice sounded through the phone, and Victoria sighed in relief.

"It's Victoria." She swallowed, realizing anew how little she and Sondra knew of each other. "I rear-ended a car."

"What? Victoria, are you all right? Was anyone hurt?"

"We're all fine, but I can't find my license or proof of insurance." Perspiration beaded on her forehead. In any other circumstance, Victoria would have never called Sondra for help. They barely knew each other. "The sheriff is taking my Suburban."

Victoria swallowed the golf ball that had formed in her throat. She couldn't begin to fathom what her one-time sister-in-law must think. Why would Sondra want to help a Thankful anyway? The family had been nothing but cruel to her.

"Oh, honey." Sondra's voice sounded smooth as silk and filled with compassion.

"He wanted me to call you to prove who I am."

"Whas madder, Mommy?" Victoria could hear the concern in her nephew's voice. She wanted so much to scoop him up and squeeze him in a big hug. She needed a hug, too.

"Everything's fine, PeeWee. Go check on your sister. Victoria, let me talk to Troy."

"Who's Troy?"

"The sheriff."

"Okay." Victoria handed him the phone. She waited as Troy smiled and talked to Sondra as if nothing had happened.

He gave it back to her. "She cleared you. I'm sorry, but you still can't have your vehicle."

Focusing on staying calm, she put the phone back to her ear. "Sondra, I'm embarrassed to ask, but is there any way you can pick me up?"

"I don't have a vehicle, Victoria. My van's in the shop, and Dylan took the truck to check on some cattle."

"Oh."

"Who's there besides Troy?"

"Uh, everyone who lives in this town is

gathered on the sidewalk, and the man I hit — I think Troy said his name was Chris."

"You hit Chris's car?"

"Yeah."

"Mary Ann?"

What is up with this car? "Yeah."

"Let me talk to him."

"What?"

"Just let me talk to him. Everything will be fine."

Victoria walked toward the man who still knelt at the rear end of his car. "I'm sorry, but my sister-in-law would like to talk to you."

He stood and took the phone. "Yeah . . . yeah . . . okay . . . okay." He handed the phone back to her. "She'd like to speak to you now."

Victoria grabbed the phone with one hand and twirled her diamond stud earring with the other. The whole ordeal had set her head to pounding in what Victoria felt sure could be considered a migraine, or at least the beginning of one. "Sondra?"

"Chris will bring you to the ranch."

"What?" She looked at the overgrown man who had turned toward Troy. Victoria watched as the sheriff nodded his head to whatever Chris had said to him. "I can't ride with him."

"Yes, you can. Trust me. He's a great guy. I'd come and get you in a heartbeat, but I can't."

"But . . ."

"Trust me. You'll be fine."

"But he hates me."

"Chris Ratliff hates no one." A crash followed by crying sounded over the phone. "Gotta go."

Victoria pushed the OFF button on her cell phone and glanced toward her ride. Chris stood with both hands shoved in his pockets. His eyes glazed and his jaw set in a hard line when he looked at her. Lifting one side of her mouth in an attempted smile, Victoria gave up the notion, walked to her Suburban, grabbed her purse, and popped open a bottle of pain reliever. She swallowed two tablets, struggling to push them down her seemingly swollen throat. Begging God to keep her from getting sick, she noted the scowling expression on Chris's face. Victoria felt confident that Sondra had no idea what she was talking about.

"Buckle up." Chris tried to sound nonchalant as he clicked his seat belt. He'd had to put his bumper in the back of Troy's cruiser as there wasn't enough room in Mary Ann for it and that gal's suitcase. Two more gigantic pieces of luggage remained in the back of her Suburban. The same two pieces he had offered to pick up and take to the ranch after he dropped off the young woman.

Is this some kind of test, Lord? His frustration with Abby had not even minimally subsided when this lady slammed into his car. Now he was chauffeuring the Mary Ann Mangler and a third of her belongings to the Wards' ranch. It didn't help matters that they were a good half hour away. He turned onto the one-lane road that could be named the longest driveway in the history of driveways. *I don't have the patience of Job.*

A glob of bird dropping hit his windshield. *Perfect. The day can't get much better.* He pulled Mary Ann to the side, opened the door, yanked his handkerchief from his back pocket, and wiped off the mess. Folding the remains into the center of the handkerchief, he carefully shoved it back into his pocket. He slid into the driver's seat and looked at his passenger peering over the suitcase resting in her lap. Her jaw had dropped, and her eyebrows had risen. Chris shrugged. "Just habit. I've been cleaning and shining this girl for eight long years." He patted the freshly oiled dashboard.

"You've fixed this car up for eight years?"

30

"Yep. She was a high school graduation present from my pa. It took me awhile to buy all the parts she needed."

"How long have you had it fixed?"

"Couple months."

She gasped. He peeked at her. She had lowered her head. "I'm truly so sorry."

Chris felt as though his heart would split in two. He knew she hadn't purposely caused the accident, and she had been so worked up about not having her license and insurance. Not that he blamed her.

He had to admit she was quite a cutie. Long, dark brown curls were pulled back in a ponytail, even though a few pieces had escaped and touched her cheek. Her profile showed the sweetest, little button nose he had ever seen. She was probably a few years younger than he, and he had to admit under different circumstances he might have taken a second look her way. "It's all right."

"No, it's not. I'll — I'll pay you back. Promise."

"We'll work it out." He started his car. In all honesty, though, he wondered what would happen if she didn't have insurance. His insurance would pay for the repairs if he wanted, but then his rates would probably go up to more than he could afford. Unless she had money.

31

He glanced at her again. She did seem to wear rather spiffy clothes. She smelled awfully good, too. If his memory served him right, Sondra's deceased husband had at one time been fairly wealthy. It seemed like his parents had disinherited him when he married Sondra. If that were true, then this lady probably did have some avenues with which to pay him back. *Then why wouldn't she have insurance?*

Of course she'd have insurance. Lots of people couldn't find the proof when they needed it. Chris shook his head. He sneaked another peek. Her head was down, her eyes closed. She seemed to be praying. Something inside him stirred, compelling him to make her feel better. "Don't worry about that citation of yours."

She looked at him; fearful innocence wrapped her face. "I've never even seen a judge."

"Henry's soft as a new puppy. You've got nothing to worry about. Show him your license and insurance, and he'll thank you and send you on your way."

"With a fine?"

Chris shrugged. "I don't know. Probably."

"That's what I thought."

She wasn't going to have insurance or cash flow. Chris could feel it. Eight years. After eight long years of fixing up Mary Ann, he'd have to stick her back in the shop and work on her a little at a time. He didn't want to think about it. Didn't need to think about it. More than anything, he just wanted to get home, eat some supper, take a hot shower, and go to bed. The sooner this day ended, the better.

CHAPTER 3

Victoria smiled as the trees cleared and Sondra's ranch came into full view. The country home screamed of serenity and coziness. "I'm so excited to meet my nephew." She twisted her purse handle around.

"You haven't met PeeWee?"

"Mother and Daddy wouldn't have any . . . Well, it's a long story."

The front door burst open. A small boy toddled out followed by Sondra holding a baby girl on her hip. Matt clapped his hands and danced around the porch. Before Chris had time to turn off the car, Victoria hopped out and ran for her nephew. She scooped him in her arms and twirled around. He squealed in delight.

"He's not afraid of me!" Victoria exclaimed as she nestled him closer to her chest.

"PeeWee isn't afraid of anyone" — Sondra laughed — "but he's been waiting for you to come. I've been showing him your picture on the refrigerator."

Happiness filled Victoria's spirit, and she hugged Sondra with her free arm. "Thank you." She turned back to her nephew and tickled his belly. "It's so good to see you" — she gazed at Sondra, willing her to fully forgive her for the years of silence — "all of you."

"You stay as long as you like. I'm glad you've come."

"Aunt Vic." Matt poked Victoria's shoulder.

"He knows my name?"

"Oh yes." Sondra tickled Matt's belly. "PeeWee's a smart boy, aren't you, Pee-Wee?"

"Boy." Matt pointed at himself.

"Yes, you are." Victoria ran her fingers through his small locks of brown hair. "You look just like your daddy."

"Daddy!" Matt squealed and leaned away from Victoria. She turned and saw a tall cowboy walking onto the porch.

"There's my little man." The cowboy took Matt from Victoria's embrace.

"Victoria, this is Dylan." Sondra pointed to the man Matt had called Daddy. A twinge of pain pricked Victoria's heart. Kenny was

Matt's daddy, not this man. She tried to push the thought aside. Kenny would want Matt to be raised by a man who would love him. According to Sondra, Dylan was a wonderful Christian man.

"Here's your bag."

Victoria turned to find Chris standing on the front lawn holding her suitcase. "I'm sorry, Chris. I'll get it."

"No, I'll take it." Dylan grabbed the bag before she could. "Swap." He handed Matt to her. Victoria hopped back onto the porch before her nephew had time to protest.

Sondra chuckled. "Come on, everyone; let's have a glass of iced tea."

"I can't stay." Chris jingled his keys and nodded toward Victoria. "I'm going to get her other two bags and bring 'em to the ranch. Then I oughta get back to Abby."

"No need to," said Dylan. "I'm going to put this suitcase in Victoria's room and then head right into town and pick up the others."

Victoria held Matt a little tighter as heat rushed up her spine. "I'm sorry for all this inconvenience."

Sondra shook her head. "Don't you worry. I needed Dylan to run to the store anyway." She turned to Chris. "Tell Abby I said to be good."

Chris grunted then nodded. "I sure will."

Victoria wondered at the odd tightness in her chest when Sondra mentioned the woman's name. She watched as Chris walked back to his car, slid inside, and then drove away. "Abby's Chris's wife?"

Dylan's boots clanked against the porch, and the door slammed as he went into the house with her suitcase. Victoria felt Sondra staring at her. Her question had come out a little more inquisitive than she had meant it to sound, so she adjusted Matt's shirt and avoided Sondra's gaze. She didn't care if Chris was married. Why would she?

"No, Abby's Chris's seventeen-year-old sister. He takes care of her."

Victoria gawked at Sondra. "Really?"

"Yeah. The girl's a little rough around the edges. Not a bad kid, really, but she gives Chris fits most of the time."

Victoria laughed. "I bet being raised by him gives Abby fits, as well."

Sondra seemed to ponder the notion. "I guess you're right. She probably needs a woman's influence." Sondra winked and walked through the front door.

Victoria didn't know if Sondra tried to imply anything, and she didn't want to think about it either. The last thing she needed was to worry about a rough-around-the-edges teenage girl.

Snuggling Matt closer, she kissed his cheek and walked into the house. It looked nothing like Victoria had imagined. Rustic femininity. Aside from the sippy cup and toy horses on the floor, Victoria felt as if she'd walked into a *Country Living* magazine. It felt so nostalgic, so homey.

"Not a four-story mansion, huh?"

Victoria jumped at Sondra's voice. "No. It's wonderful."

Cocking her head, Sondra seemed to study her. Finally she smiled. "Would you like a glass of iced tea, or do you want to unpack first?"

"I think I'd like to go ahead and unpack."

"Sure thing." Sondra pointed down the hall. "Your room is the first one on the left. Dylan's already put your luggage in there."

"Thanks." Victoria put her precious nephew on the floor next to his horses. "I'll be back to play with you in just a minute." She caressed his chin. *I wish I had seen him as a newborn, held him, kissed him, spoiled him.* She sighed and then stood. "Thank you, Sondra, for letting me come. I wish . . ." Victoria's voice cracked, and she knew at any moment she'd have to allow herself a good, long cry.

"Get yourself on to your room. I'll get the

tea, plus a batch of cookies I just made up. Unpack a bit, and then we'll talk."

Victoria nodded and headed down the hall. *Sondra is a wonderful person. Mother and Daddy were wrong. So wrong.*

"Tell me that you did not burn lunch." The stench of burned eggs filled the room. Chris waved his hand through the layer of smoke above the stove. He peered into the living area connected to their kitchen and saw Abby lounging in the recliner with her back to one of its arms and her legs draped over the other. She wore her fluffy house shoes that were caked with mud from tromping back and forth to the garden. Instead of stomping the mess off outside or even in the mudroom, clumps of earth had fallen on the floor beneath her feet.

"Hang on a sec." Abby covered the phone with her hand. "I didn't aim to, Chris. The phone rang, and well, I've been cleaning it up."

Chris glared at the partly scraped skillet sitting in the sink. Abby hadn't even put soapy water in it. She'd just left it there. He supposed she thought animated farm animals came in and cleaned up irresponsible teenagers' messes. "Get off that phone."

"But . . ."

"Now." The fact that she had the audacity to be talking on the phone after driving the truck without asking, smashing the mailbox, and burning lunch made Chris's blood boil.

"I gotta go. My brother's about to flip out on me."

Chris gritted his teeth. He had every right to be angry with her, yet she continued to be openly disrespectful and didn't seem to care a bit.

"One year, and I'm gone." Abby clicked off the phone and folded her arms in front of her chest. "Go ahead. Lay it on, *big brother*. It ain't like I meant to burn the eggs."

That was it. He'd had it. "Abby, you are grounded for a month. No TV. No phone. No friends. Nothing."

"But, brudder . . ."

"No buts."

"You're going to ground me the summer before my senior year?" Her voice resonated calm, controlled. Chris had learned this tone, the let's-talk-reasonably one that somehow always seemed to land Abby with whatever she wanted.

"Yes, I am."

"Now, brother, let's be reasonable." She spoke softly as she turned on the kitchen faucet. "I will clean this up a bit, and then

40

we'll talk."

Chris did not miss the sarcasm that dripped from her lips. She intended to manipulate the situation in such a way that he became the bad guy. He pressed his car key against his lips, allowing its coolness to keep his temper in check. "You will clean this up, but you are still grounded."

"Now, Chris . . ."

He shook his head. "I'm not changing my mind, Abby."

She huffed, and her lips formed a straight line. He could see she was about to lose her composure when she smacked the countertop. "You're just . . . just an overgrown meanie."

"And you're still grounded." He walked out of the house and slammed the door. He wasn't even hungry anymore. Stalking to the garage, he pulled a paper and pen from his coveralls. He'd just assess the damage to Mary Ann. If he never saw another female in his life, that would be too soon.

"I'm too tired to unpack." Victoria flopped on top of the bed. She stared at the stucco, flower-looking pattern on the ceiling. Exhaustion claimed every inch of her being. The very thought of putting her clothes and accessories away seemed incomprehensible.

She willed herself to sit up on the bed. *I don't have to do everything today. Talk to Sondra, yes, but unpacking can wait until tomorrow.* She opened her suitcase to freshen up her makeup and brush her hair before going to the kitchen. Her license fell onto the bed. "I can't believe it."

Picking it up, she remembered Ms. Ginny had found it underneath the microwave when she was cleaning. She had given it to Victoria just before she left for her new job. Upset about losing the woman who'd been working for the Thankful family since before Kenny's birth, Victoria simply pitched it in the suitcase and hugged the dear, older woman one last time.

"If I don't get my head on straight, I'll never be able to take care of myself." She peered in the mirror above her new dresser. Curly wisps had escaped her ponytail. Most of her makeup had worn off from the long drive. She looked like she was about sixteen. Grabbing her hairbrush, she pulled the elastic band out of her hair and brushed out her curls. She covered her freckles with powder again. "That's a little better."

Straightening her shoulders, she lifted her chin and stared at her reflection. "You can do this." The knot tightened in her belly as she opened the bedroom door and walked down the hall. She had a lot to talk about, and she had no idea how her sister-in-law would react. "Sondra?"

"In here," Sondra called from Victoria's left.

"Hey." Victoria felt shy as she joined her sister-in-law at the massive wooden table in the kitchen/dining area. True to her word, Sondra had cookies and iced tea waiting for her.

"I went ahead and laid the kids down for a nap. I wanted us to have a chance to talk."

"Okay." Victoria's heart sank. She wanted so much to play with Matt, yet she knew they needed to have this time.

Sondra pointed to the plate. "Have one. Is chocolate chip your favorite just like your brother?"

"Yeah. Grams used to make them for us." She took a small bite and gasped. "Sondra, these taste just like Grams's."

Sondra smiled. "I know. They're her recipe. She taught me how to make them for Kenny while we were dating." She looked Victoria in the eye. "I loved your brother very much."

Victoria gawked at the woman sitting across the table from her. Tears welled in Victoria's eyes. Why had she waited so long to come here? She knew why. Fear. Fear of

43

her daddy disowning her just as he had Kenny. Fear of not being able to make it on her own.

And what did all that fear get me? The last weeks of Kenny's life — missed. The first two years of Matt's life — missed. A real relationship with her sister-in-law — missed. *Forgive me, Lord. I should have trusted in You. Bless my relationship with Sondra and Matt now.*

Victoria wiped the tears from her eyes. "I'm sorry I missed all this time with you."

Sondra touched the top of Victoria's hand. "It's all right. We can start now. I'm glad you're here." She leaned back in her chair. "Seeing you brings a wave of sweet memories to my mind. I still miss Kenny at times."

"What about Dylan?"

"I love Dylan completely. Kenny was a part of my life. He still is, in the form of his son. My life and heart are committed to Dylan, but I still remember and love your brother." Sondra stopped. "Kenny would approve of Dylan."

Victoria nodded. "I believe you're right. He seems to be a wonderful man."

Sondra smiled. "Okay, now that that's cleared, how long are you going to visit? Victoria, we want you to stay as long as you can. . . ." She touched the top of Victoria's hand. "But I don't want to make things hard on you. If your dad wants you home, don't worry about hurting my feelings. I understand. . . ."

"You don't have to worry about that."

Sondra's eyebrows furrowed. "I don't?"

Victoria shook her head and tried to conjure the courage to tell Sondra the truth. *Just spit it out.* "Sondra . . . well . . . it appears I can stay as long as you'll have me, or at least until I can get a job and an apartment."

"What?"

Victoria twisted her napkin between her fingers. The stunned expression on Sondra's face did not make telling the truth any easier. Victoria had lived her entire existence in an abundance of wealth. Admitting her state of destitution proved far more difficult than she had imagined. *Get on with it.* "It seems my daddy hasn't always managed his affairs in completely legal ways."

Victoria's tongue stuck to the roof of her mouth. She took a long drink of tea. She couldn't taste it; she only felt the cool liquid flow down the back of her throat. No matter how many gulps she took, she still felt parched.

"Just tell me. You'll feel better once it's out."

Victoria set the glass on the table. "You're right." She swallowed. "It seems Daddy embezzled a good deal of money from his company. He claims to be innocent, yet he and Mom flew to who-knows-where to get away from the law."

She closed her eyes. She couldn't look at Sondra. "Everything belongs to the government until Daddy goes to court. What I have with me is all I own in the world." Her bottom lip quivered. "I have to make it alone. I don't have any money. Now I've hit a man's special car. I pray my insurance will take care of it."

Victoria felt Sondra's arms wrap around her. "I want you to stay with us for as long as you need. I don't want you to even think of going anywhere else. You are welcome here."

Fresh tears streamed down Victoria's face. The day had been entirely too emotional. The long drive only aided her exhaustion and feelings of helplessness. Victoria hugged her sister-in-law in return. "Thank you, Sondra. I wish I had come years ago. I wish I could turn back time."

"The past has passed. We have today and all of the tomorrows the Lord gives us."

"That's true . . ."

A man cleared his throat behind her. Vic-

46

toria wiped her eyes with a napkin as Sondra looked around her and said, "Hi, Chris. Back so soon?"

Knowing her face was a blotchy mess, Victoria prayed he would leave quickly so she wouldn't have to acknowledge him.

Metal jingled in his pocket. "Dylan called. Seems Jeff needed some help on the ranch right away. He asked me to go and get Victoria's other suitcases for him."

Victoria closed her eyes and exhaled. She would have to turn around and talk to him. He would see the red blotches she knew covered her eyes like a raccoon. He'd see the freckles that splattered her face. If her guess was right, he'd also see mascara streaming down her cheeks. *Why did I have to start crying?*

Knowing etiquette demanded she thank the person who had just made a special trip to bring her luggage, she turned and stood slowly to face Chris. Looking up at the towering figure, she nodded and said, "Thank you, Chris. I'll show you where to put them."

He followed her to the bedroom. She stood in the door as he placed both suitcases on the floor. Her heart beat faster when their gazes locked through the mirror above the dresser. He didn't turn to face her but

47

continued to stare in the mirror.

"Did I scare you?" His voice was barely audible.

"What?"

"Earlier today. Did I scare you?"

"No." She frowned. "Why would you think that?"

"I'm big, and I can come across as gruff; I can see you've been . . ."

"Crying." Victoria finished his sentence. "No. That has nothing to do with you." Embarrassment washed over her, but she couldn't take her gaze from his. Something about the overgrown, grease-covered man drew her. She wanted to tell him all that had happened. Wanted to hear him say that everything would be okay.

She peered out the window. *What is wrong with me?* She didn't know this man, not the first thing about him. For all she knew, he was a horrible criminal. *No, Sondra wouldn't have let him bring me to her house if that were true.*

She glanced back at the mirror. He still stood looking at her. She lifted her chin and pushed away from the door. "Well, thank you, Chris."

He moved closer until he loomed more than a foot over her. "You're welcome."

Her chest tightened, and Victoria felt she'd

soon be gasping for air. She lifted her shoulders and took long, slow breaths, willing herself not to come undone in front of this stranger. "Be sure to let me know how much I'll owe you for the damages."

"Oh, I will."

Victoria stepped away from the intensity of his gaze. He walked down the hall, nodded toward Sondra, and then went out the door. Victoria grabbed her chest, watching as he took long strides toward his truck. She had no idea what had just happened, but she felt fairly confident that whatever it was it wasn't good.

CHAPTER 4

A hint of sunlight streamed through Victoria's window. Glancing at the alarm clock beside her bed, she gasped at the early hour. She slipped out from under her covers and slinked into her robe and slippers. Stretching her arms above her head, Victoria yawned and then rubbed sleep from her eyes. She stumbled to the window just in time to see the sun finish its ascent into the expansive heavens. *Oh, Lord, Your handiwork is amazing.*

Deep green pastures extended as far as she could see. The sky lifted bright and full above her. It reminded her of the enclosure and privacy she felt as a small girl when she would make a fort with extra blankets from her closet, and yet the sky was not in any way private. It was vast and clear and awesome.

The bedroom door creaked open. Sondra stuck her head inside and smiled. "You're up. Great! I came to see if you wanted to gather eggs with me."

Victoria smiled and tried to imagine what gathering eggs could possibly be like. Would she have to touch the chickens? Victoria had always heard they were quite disgusting creatures, but then most animals were a bit on the yucky side. "Sure, but what does a gal wear to gather eggs?"

Sondra giggled quietly. "On a warm day like today, a gal wears a pair of shorts and a T-shirt." She wrinkled her nose. "Course, the chickens just might be offended if you don't match."

Feigning hurt, Victoria rested her hands on her hips. "Are you making fun of me?"

"Yes. Now hurry before the kids wake up, and I'll show you around the ranch."

Victoria grinned and shut the door. She unzipped her suitcase and rummaged for a pair of casual shorts. "Note to self," she murmured as she tossed one article after the other onto the bed, "I must unpack first thing after breakfast." She picked up a silk shirt and wrinkled her nose. "And find some ranch-appropriate items." Sighing, she decided on a pair of jean shorts and a designer button-down shirt. *At least I have some old tennis shoes.* After scooping them up from the closet floor, she put them on, tied her shoelaces, and hopped off the bed.

The thought of being around live, squawking chickens made her stomach churn, but she had determined to make the best of it. In truth, part of her was excited about learning the life of a country girl. Walking to the window, she glanced once more at the chunk of nature that lay all around her. She spotted the pigsty and its enormous inhabitants and snarled. *It's a small part of me, that's for sure.*

Victoria walked out of her bedroom and down the hall. Too tempted to just pass by, she peeked into Matt's room. Her precious nephew lay in his toddler bed holding a small, flannel-squared blanket close to his face. *Kenny had a favorite shirt that color.* She touched the corner of her mouth. *I wonder . . .*

Tiptoeing closer to Matt, she noted how his small blanket had been hand-stitched and not store-bought. Softly brushing his cheek, she whispered, "I'll have to ask your mommy." She sighed at how peaceful he appeared. Quietly closing the door, Victoria tiptoed down the hall and out the front door.

A warm breeze whipped her hair, escorting with it the strong odor of cattle grazing nearby. Victoria frowned and covered her nose.

"The smell actually starts to grow on you." Sondra came from behind her.

"You scared the life out of me." Victoria placed her hand on her chest to calm her now fast-beating heart.

"Sorry." Sondra handed Victoria an empty basket and then hefted her own higher onto her forearm. "I hated the smell out here at first. Believe it or not, now I actually look forward to it when I'm coming home from town or wherever."

Victoria wrinkled her nose. "Really?"

Sondra nodded. "Yeah. It's a funny thing what living in the country will do for you after a while."

Victoria didn't respond, and Sondra turned and headed toward what Victoria assumed was a chicken coop. In actuality it looked like a rather fun, oversized playhouse. Sporting a door and latticed windows in the front, the entire building was painted white and trimmed in country blue. Sondra walked around the back and pointed to the wire-fenced "yard" for the chickens. A small ramp connected the ground and the opening of the building. Several chickens squawked around the yard.

"We have a lot of chickens," Sondra said.

"I love to take the baby chicks to the Lawton Group Home to let the children hold them."

"That's wonderful." Victoria tried to count the chickens but soon had to give up due to their scurrying around. Walking back around the building, Sondra opened the door and went inside. Victoria braced herself for an attack of white-feathered beasts. To her surprise, nothing happened.

"Come on in. There's plenty of room," Sondra called.

"Actually, I have a question about Matt." Victoria grasped her basket. There was no way she intended to go inside that little building with all those creatures. Visions of chickens pecking her feet and pulling at her shoelaces filled her mind. *Can chickens fly?* Victoria shuddered as she imagined them flying around her and plucking at her hair.

Sondra opened the door wide. "What are you waiting for?" She motioned for Victoria to join her. "So what's your question?"

"Well, I noticed . . ." Victoria stopped when she saw several squares sitting three by three against the wall. Fencing seemed to separate the chickens from the humans. Slowly Victoria stepped inside. She watched as her sister-in-law unlatched and opened a section behind one of the squares.

Sondra scooped an egg from the nest. "See, not as bad as you thought." Sondra showed the egg to Victoria and then placed it in her basket. "You get the next one. Nothing's going to get you."

Determined not to act like a spoiled rich girl, Victoria swallowed and opened a second square. Pulling the egg from the nest, she held it up. "I did it." She placed the egg in her basket and commenced to collect more eggs.

"You'll be just fine." Sondra grabbed a bag of feed from beside her. Victoria watched as she filled a large can that had an opening on the other side of the fence. In a matter of moments, the chickens' feed spilled out in front of them. "So what did you notice about PeeWee?"

Victoria turned toward Sondra. "His blanket."

Sondra exhaled. "It's made from Kenny's shirts."

"I thought so."

"It's a little piece of Kenny that Matt can hold on to. When he grows older, I plan to put it away and give it to him when he's grown."

Victoria's chin quivered as her emotions threatened to get the best of her once more. "I'm so grateful for you."

Sondra furrowed her eyebrows. "What?"

"Kenny was blessed to have you, even though your time together was short. I know you made his last months wonderful."

"I hope so. I want PeeWee to know who his father was and that Kenny loved him." She looked at Victoria. "Dylan and I both want that."

"I'm glad."

Sondra hooked her arm with Victoria's. "Before we continue our tour, why don't we head to the house and get breakfast started?"

Victoria's stomach grumbled. "Sounds good to me."

Feeling as inept in the kitchen as she had in the chicken coop, Victoria did little more than watch as Sondra rolled biscuits, fried bacon, scrambled eggs, and mixed gravy. Being given the seemingly simple task of cracking eggs, Victoria had even botched that by dropping as much shell as egg into the skillet.

"You'll learn." Sondra had tried to encourage her. "Just takes time."

Victoria didn't feel encouraged. She felt like a poor excuse for a person. The things she was good at, like shopping, cosmetology, and hairstyles, were not practical for everyday, real-world living. She could hold her own at movie and television trivia, as well, but that didn't help here on the farm either.

Matt woke up, scampered into the kitchen, and wrapped his arms around Sondra's leg. "I tirsy, Mommy."

Victoria smiled at the patch of curls that fell into his eyes. He shook his head and swiped them away.

"I bet Aunt Victoria will get you a drink of juice." Sondra unwrapped his arms from her leg and pushed him toward Victoria.

"Come on, little buddy." She extended her arms, and he scampered into them. Lifting him to her chest, Victoria nestled her nose against his soft cheek. *How could I have spent so long away from you?*

"Juice, Aunt Vic, juice!" Matt grabbed a handful of hair and pulled.

"No, Matt." Sondra turned and scolded him. "Do not pull hair. Say please."

Matt frowned and stuck out his little bottom lip. Victoria thought she would melt. The child could have her hair, the whole head full. She didn't want to be the cause of his tears first thing in the morning. Victoria tickled his chin, and he smiled. "Pwease."

"A gal can't resist that." She grabbed the sippy cup Sondra had set on the counter,

57

opened the refrigerator, and, with one arm still holding Matt, managed to pour the juice and attach the lid.

"Pretty good for a first timer." Dylan walked into the room, and Matt squealed and practically launched himself toward the man he called *Daddy.*

"Come here, PeeWee." Dylan grabbed him out of Victoria's arms and then tossed him in the air like a play toy. "You gonna help Daddy feed the horses?"

Matt giggled and nodded his head. A needle still pricked Victoria's heart that Kenny wasn't the one taking Matt to feed the horses. Logically, she was happy Matt would have a father to take care of him, but emotionally, Victoria longed to see Kenny with his son. *God, Kenny would have been such a good dad.*

"Dylan's a great dad." Sondra's words interrupted Victoria's thoughts.

"I can see that."

Sondra scooped the scrambled eggs into a serving bowl. "Did you know Dylan was with me when PeeWee was born?"

"No." Victoria transferred the fresh-from-the-oven biscuits from the baking sheet to a plate.

"He was. Dylan took care of me when Kenny couldn't. It's probably hard for you

58

to see Dylan and Matt together, but he's proof of God's mercy and blessings to me and Matt. Even to Kenny."

Victoria gazed at Sondra. She couldn't imagine how it could possibly be a blessing to Kenny.

"Kenny wouldn't have wanted me to struggle alone."

Victoria sighed. She gazed out the kitchen window and saw Matt scampering as quickly as he could behind Dylan. He struggled to carry a sack, a smaller version of the one Dylan held. No doubt it was the feed for the horses. Even from a distance, Victoria could see Matt's happiness at getting to help his daddy.

In that instant, Victoria felt a peace, a *real* peace. Sondra was right. God had been merciful. He had blessed Sondra, Matt, and even Kenny. Matt was under the tutelage of a man who helped bring him into the world. Kenny would be happy.

"I need to tell you something, Victoria."

Victoria looked at Sondra who was wringing water viciously out of a dishrag and into the sink. "What?"

Sondra pointed to a chair. "You may want to have a seat."

"I'm okay." Bile rose in Victoria's throat. Something was about to happen. Something monumental. Again. Victoria didn't know if she could take many more surprises in her life.

"A friend of mine is in the insurance business." Sondra sighed. "I called her last night and asked her if there was any way she could find out who your dad had his insurance with."

Victoria slunk down into a chair and plastered a fake smile to her lips. "Yes?"

"My friend had already heard about your dad's, uh, situation. He's fairly well-known. Many people vied for his services." Sondra wiped splattered milk and egg drippings from the counter. She turned and eyed Victoria. "I might as well just say it. Your dad's insurance policies weren't paid up when he left the country."

"What are you saying?"

Sondra placed her hand on Victoria's shoulder. "What I'm saying is, you don't have any insurance."

Chris unscrewed the top to his truck's gas tank. After selecting the cheaper unleaded gas, he shoved the nozzle into the tank and started to fill up the truck.

"How's your car?"

Chris turned and saw Mandy Reynolds filling up at the pump beside him. "Needin'

60

some work."

"I heard." Mandy smacked her free hand to her hip. Her two young sons in the back-seat began to squabble over a toy. "Roland came home from the vet's office last night. Said he saw the whole thing and that the girl wasn't paying a bit of attention."

Chris cringed. He tried to keep a low profile in this "Mayberry" town. He hated being the topic of conversation, especially after the rumors that had gone around when his ma had up and decided to leave. He and Abby still dealt with the hurt that resulted from the townsfolk's talk.

"Virginia called me last night, too. Said the gal was just a hoity-toity, young thing. Came running through the town like she owned the place. Virginia said that girl wasn't the least bit sorry for ruining that wonderful car you spent all that time fixing up." Mandy turned toward her sons whose squabble had escalated to an all-out, fist-flinging war. "Give me that toy. Neither one of you gets it."

Chris released the handle to the pump and pulled it away from the tank. Glad he'd used his debit card, all he had to do was screw on the cap and he could go.

"I don't know who these young gals think they are these days," Mandy continued, "thinking they can go around slamming into people's cars. . . ."

"It was an accident, Mandy," Chris interrupted her. "She was sorry. It could happen to anyone." With a nod of his head, he jumped in the truck and added, "Have a good day." He started the engine and drove toward the ranch. He hoped Victoria didn't plan on staying too long. If he was having a conversation like that this early in the morning, then Victoria would have a hard way to go around here.

He glanced at the paper on the passenger's seat beside him. He'd figured a very fair — actually quite low — price. Her insurance company shouldn't have a problem with it, especially once they saw the pictures he had taken last night. The fact that he would do the labor for free should also help keep her rates down a bit.

Pulling into the ranch, he couldn't seem to get a handle on the sinking feeling that seemed to plague his gut. *Probably just the burned biscuits and undercooked eggs from breakfast this morning.* Abby had awakened still miffed over her one-month grounding, but Chris had stuck to his guns. He had spoken nicely to her but hadn't budged on the punishment.

Chris shut off the engine, grabbed the

paper, and opened the truck door just as Victoria opened the screen with a coffee cup in her hand.

"Chris?" Her eyes widened in surprise. "We just finished the breakfast dishes, but I'm sure Sondra won't mind if I find you something to eat. . . ."

"I'm fine. Already eaten." Chris smiled. Either country hospitality had already begun to rub off on her, or she genuinely had a sweet turn. Taking in the truth and sincerity radiating from her light eyes and remembering her silent prayer in his car the day before, Chris decided to believe the latter assumption. "I just came to pick up the eggs for the food bank. Brought some milk, too."

Victoria frowned. "Food bank? Milk?"

"Yeah, we swap. I bring Sondra milk, and she donates her extra eggs to families in the county who need them."

"That doesn't surprise me at all. You take them for her?"

"A few years back when my pa was still living, he came up with a ministry to take the eggs to the bank, as well as distributing them to those who couldn't get out."

Victoria wrapped both hands around the coffee cup and peered into the sky. "Sounds like your dad was as giving a person as Sondra."

"Yep, true about both of them."

She glanced back at him. "But why does your truck say BY HIS HAND on the side?"

"My sister was so excited about Pa's ministry that she wanted to give it a name. Once we decided on one, she and I painted the letters on Pa's older work truck."

The memory of his sister and him working all day one Saturday to paint the letters drifted into his mind. They'd gotten into a paint fight, and by the time they'd finished, they were covered in blue and red splotches from the tops of their heads to their toes. Abby'd had blue paint splatters in her hair for weeks afterward.

Victoria sighed, forcing Chris from his memories. "I don't know what I'd do without Sondra right now."

Unsure of where this conversation was headed and confused by the winsome tone in her voice, Chris cleared his throat and scuffed his shoes along the dirt. "Yes, well . . ."

"Anyway." Victoria placed the cup on the porch railing and wiped her hand on her shorts. Her neck and cheeks blazed red. "Can I help you load them or anything?"

"No, she always has them boxed and ready

by the coop." He pointed toward the building.

"Oh." Victoria furrowed her brow. "I helped her with that this morning and didn't even realize what we were doing."

Her sincerity struck Chris as funny, and he laughed. "It's all new to you, huh?"

Victoria shrugged and smiled, exposing straight teeth, whiter than he'd ever seen. "Yep, but I'm enjoying it." Her light eyes danced as she scanned the land around him. "I think I could get used to all this. I've never seen so much green and blue in all my life."

Chris followed her gaze and wondered if he took nature's beauty for granted. Looking back at Victoria and the childlike awe in her expression, he knew he did.

"Do you think God likes blue and green the best?"

"I'm not sure."

"Have you ever noticed how so much of nature is colored in some shade of the two? I'd never realized it before."

"Can't say that I've paid much attention either." Chris smiled and stepped closer to the porch, feeling drawn to her innocence. For a moment, he wanted to see things from her eyes. He wanted to get to know her more, to find out what she was thinking and what made her think that way. He wanted to ask how her heart felt about the God he served. Could she be as sold out as he wanted to be?

She blushed again and backed up toward the door. "I'm sorry. Sometimes I say the silliest things. I better go and see if Sondra needs any help."

Knocked back into reality, Chris shook his head and looked down at the figures he held. "I also wanted to give you the estimate for fixing my car."

Her expression fell, and her eyes clouded. "O–kay."

The weight lodged in his gut again, seeming to hold his breath beneath it. Something strong and fierce told him that she would not be able to pay to fix Mary Ann, and he would spend the next two or three years raising the money to do it himself.

Sondra walked out onto the porch. "Chris, how nice to see you. Come on inside."

Chris shook his head. "I just came to bring you some milk and pick up the eggs for the food bank. Give Victoria my figures, as well." He handed the paper to Victoria. "They're low. I only put the cost of parts on there since I'll do the labor myself. Your insurance company shouldn't have a problem."

"O–kay." Victoria took the paper from him. Her eyes widened as she scanned the page.

Sondra nudged her shoulder. "You need to tell him."

Chris looked from Sondra to Victoria. Victoria's eyes welled with emotion for a moment, but she quickly blinked it away. Something in him longed to touch her cheek and tell her everything would be all right. He shook his head. He didn't even know the woman, except that she was a disaster waiting to happen. And he could sense the wait was about to end . . . again.

Victoria glanced at her sister-in-law.

"Just be honest with him. He's a great guy," Sondra whispered. She turned to Chris. "I've gotta check on the kids. I'll let you two talk."

Victoria glanced at Chris. The snarl on his face compared to that of a bulldog. She just couldn't quite see the "great guy" Sondra kept talking about. Every time Victoria spoke with him, it was under a large amount of tension. Admittedly, tension caused by her, but it made her nervous nonetheless.

"So what's going on?" Chris said the words with what could only be described as vehement dread.

Victoria inhaled and straightened her shoulders. She would not feel inferior to this man. The accident was her fault. Her circumstances were not. She would do what she could, in whatever way she could, to make things right. After all, she had the Creator of the universe to turn to for guidance, and He never failed her. She smiled. "Would you like to have a seat?" She pointed to one of the rocking chairs on the porch. Lifting her cup, she added, "Maybe a cup of coffee?"

Chris frowned, and the snarl deepened. *The Dukes of Hazzard* hunk had transformed into a red-eyed bull whose gaze targeted on her. Victoria looked down to see what she'd chosen to wear this morning. Noting the crimson color, she wished she'd chosen more calming attire.

"No, thank you. Just tell me what you have to say."

He did add a "thank-you" to the "no," which encouraged her. Maybe he would take her news better than she'd anticipated. *Just spit it out and get it over with.* "It seems I don't have insurance. My daddy didn't renew our policy, and I didn't know it."

Chris lowered himself into one of the rocking chairs. He closed his eyes and exhaled. She watched as his Adam's apple bobbed up and down in an effort to control what he must be feeling.

Okay, so maybe he's taking it exactly as I expected. She sat in the chair beside him.

"All those years. All that saving," Chris mumbled.

"I am sorry. I'll do whatever I can. . . ."

"Are you?" Chris's eyes opened, and he sat up straight. "Well, that's wonderful. You come storming into town, smashing my car with no insurance, but you're nice and sorry." He stood and stomped off the porch. "I'm *so* glad you're sorry."

Victoria jumped out of the chair and walked to him. She stood to her full height even though he still towered over her. Lifting her chin, she glared at him. "I will still pay for your *precious* Mary Ann."

"That's good. It's the least you could do. After all, it's your mess . . ." He pointed at his chest. "And I'm fixing it."

"Go on home, Mr. Ratliff." Victoria stomped away from him. Reaching the porch, she turned to face him. She touched her finger to her other palm. "The money is as good as in your hand."

Chris jumped in his truck, growled with the engine, and drove away.

She bit the inside of her lip. "Now how am I going to go about doing that?"

CHAPTER 5

Victoria looked away from the pawnshop owner and down at the ring one last time. It had been a priceless treasure to her grandmother. Her grandfather had died before Victoria was born, and Grams had often told her stories of their courtship.

"My daddy used to chase your grandpa off the porch each time he came around." Victoria could hear Grams's voice and her tongue clicking as if she were in the room with her.

"But your grandpa would come back the next day anyway." She had laughed. "Used to drive my daddy crazy."

Victoria would nestle into her grandmother's lap and close her eyes as Grams combed her fingers through Victoria's hair. "But your grandpa and I were crazy in love."

Victoria touched the small, round diamond resting in a square setting. Smaller diamonds made their home on each side. In truth, the ring wasn't much to look at, but it had always been precious, first to her grandmother, and since her death, to Victoria.

"You know, I really don't mind loaning you a little money to help get you started," Dylan leaned over and whispered in her ear.

Victoria flashed a smile at the oversized cowboy. He'd really grown on her in the last few days. "I can't let you do that."

"Pride isn't always a good thing, Vic."

Victoria sighed, gazing back at the ring. "It's really not about pride. I've never had to work for anything. Never had to lose anything." She peered up at Dylan. "I'm spoiled. I always have been. I don't know if I can fully explain it to you, but I have to do this on my own."

Dylan wrapped his arm around her shoulder and gave her a quick squeeze. "You're all right, Vic. You're gonna be just fine."

With that, Victoria quickly handed the ring to the pawnshop owner and grabbed the offered money off the counter. "You'll keep my ring for one month, before anyone can buy it?"

"Yes, ma'am." The man smiled, exposing a missing front tooth. He didn't appear like someone to be trusted, according to every television program Victoria had ever seen, but Dylan promised that the man ran a legitimate business.

"Are we ready?" Victoria forced a smile.

"Whenever you are."

"Let's go." Victoria turned toward the door and bumped into an even larger figure. "Oh, excuse me." She glanced at her feet and tried to walk around.

"Victoria, what are you doing here?" She looked up at the sound of the familiar voice and watched as Chris extended his hand to Dylan. "Well, hello, Dylan."

Victoria exhaled and crossed her arms in front of her chest. *This is just great.*

"Dylan, I don't reckon I've ever seen you in here before." Chris shook hands with his friend. "You don't play any instruments on the sly, do you?"

Dylan shook his head and waved his hands. "Oh no."

"Buying some jewelry for Sondra?" Chris glanced at Victoria. Her eyes had doubled their size, and she appeared as if she might keel over. "You okay?"

"Just running some errands," answered Dylan. "So what are you doing here?"

"Looking at guitars." The color in Victoria's face returned. He wondered if he'd scared her when he stormed off the other

72

morning. He probably needed to apologize. Never would he want a woman, or anyone for that matter, to be afraid of him. "Victoria, I'm sorry if I scared you the other day."

"Vic's all right. She's a tough ol' gal," added Dylan.

Chris frowned at Dylan. He was acting mighty strangely. Glancing at Victoria, Chris smiled. "You go by Vic?"

She shrugged and half smiled. "PeeWee gave me the name."

"I'm not sure if you look like a Vic. You're young. Innocent. With a bit of fire." Her eyes widened, and Chris laughed. "Yeah. I guess it suits you just fine."

Victoria lifted her chin. "So what was it you said you were doing here, Chris?"

He gazed down at his guitar and the music papers in his hand. "I love to sing worship at church, but my guitar has just about given out. It'd still be good for someone who likes to fiddle around a little bit, but it won't make it much longer being used three times a week and then whenever I feel a drawing to her in the evenings."

"Does your guitar have a name, as well?"

Chris laughed out loud. "As a matter of fact, she does." He lifted the guitar toward Victoria. "Vic, this is Belle. Belle, this is Vic.

I'm sorry you won't get to know each other much as I'm getting ready to trade in Belle, but you've been introduced just the same."

"Do you trade in your girls often?"

"Not the ones worth keeping." Victoria's neck and cheeks turned crimson as she looked away. He hadn't meant anything by his words. Did she think he spoke of her? Chris drank in her whole image, as well as considered her fiery spirit that mingled with sincerity and truth. If Victoria Thankful was anything, she was definitely worth keeping. "I don't think that came out . . ."

"Well, there you have it." Dylan interrupted. He grabbed Victoria's arm. "We best get going. Sondra's expecting us back soon."

"Okay." Chris waved, feeling confident he'd made a total fool of himself. "I'll see you at church on Sunday. Hope to see you there, Vic."

Dylan and Victoria walked toward the door. She leaned closer to him and whispered, "What did he mean by that?"

Dylan shook his head. "Not a thing, darlin'. Don't go overanalyzing the things men say. Sondra makes me crazy when she does that."

Chris closed his eyes at the overheard conversation. He had hurt her feelings, but there was nothing he could do about it now.

Frustrated, he turned and walked to the counter. "Hey, Vern. My guitar needs a bit of updating. Think we can make up a deal?"

"I'd reckon." The man pointed to the guitars hanging on the wall. "Pick out what you want, and we'll see what we can do."

Chris selected the one that would suit his need but wouldn't be too expensive. He set it on the counter and counted out the amount Vern wanted for the trade. "I was wondering. . . ." He handed the money to Vern. "Did that man and woman who were just in here buy anything?"

Vern shook his head. "Nah. She just wanted to pawn a ring." He sighed. "She had a hard time parting with it." He handed the change to Chris. "If people would learn to pay with cash instead of credit, they wouldn't have to give up the treasures they love." The man clicked his tongue. "Course, then I wouldn't be in business."

Chris placed the change in his billfold and put it in his back pocket. "Could I see the ring she brought in?"

"Sure." Vern grabbed a tray from underneath the counter.

Chris picked up the ring. It was actually kind of small, not something he would have expected Victoria to wear. *Why would she want to pawn this small ring?*

"That little ring there is actually worth a nice piece of money. It's a perfect diamond, and they don't make settings like that anymore. Sure, someone could try, but there's detailing to it that proves the ring's age."

Chris put the ring on the tip of his pinky finger.

"Said it was her grandma's," Vern added.

So it was important to her. Chris didn't understand his need to help the woman who had banged into his life and turned it upside down, but he couldn't deny the desire was there. Each time he peered into her honest eyes, he wanted to confess a million feelings, though he still couldn't quite put his finger on what they were. "How much do you want for it?"

The man shook his head. "I promised her I'd keep it a month, and you know I'm a man of my word."

Chris picked up his guitar. "Yep, you are, and I'm glad of it."

"Tell you what I can do." Vern slid a piece of paper and a pencil in front of Chris. "Give me your number, and I'll give you a call if she doesn't get here in a month."

Chris grinned. "I'd appreciate that."

Victoria walked through the door and

scooped her excited nephew off the floor. "I miss you, Vic."

"I missed you, too, PeeWee."

She hugged him close, inhaling the sweet baby-shampoo scent that lingered in his soft brown curls. "Where's your mama?"

Matt struggled for her to put him down. She did, and he grabbed her hand, pulling her toward the kitchen. "Come. I sew you."

"So how'd it go?" Sondra sat Emily in her high chair and belted her in. She popped open a jar of bananas and grabbed a baby spoon from the drawer. "Oh, I forgot her bib. Will you get one for me?"

Victoria took one from the drawer and fastened it around Emily's neck. Leaning over, she gave her a kiss on her cheek before the child's face became a World War II battle zone covered in mushy bananas.

"I think I got enough to get my Suburban back, pay for three months of insurance, and even cover the court expense. Hopefully it will be small."

"That's wonderful." Sondra opened her mouth to coax Emily to do so, as well. When she did, Sondra shoved a spoonful inside. Emily laughed as she blew it back out. "The little stink. She thinks this is a game."

Victoria laughed. "It is." She sobered and sat in a chair beside her sister-in-law.

Sondra wiped Emily's mouth. "What's wrong, Vic?"

"I can't pay Chris."

"Dylan and I will be happy to loan you the money."

"You know I can't take it." She folded her arm over the back of the chair and gazed out the kitchen window above the sink. "I thought God wouldn't give us more than we can handle, and, Sondra, I just don't think I can handle any more."

"Nope." Sondra popped a glob of bananas in Emily's mouth and smacked her lips together in an effort to get her little one to do the same. Instead Emily giggled and allowed the mush to run down her chin. Sondra groaned. "That's not what the Bible says."

"What?" Victoria turned and gawked at her sister-in-law. "Yes, it does. I remember reading it." She watched as Sondra made the spoon into a mock airplane and zoomed it around Emily's face until it landed in her mouth.

"Nope. The Bible says that no temptation will be greater than what we can bear because God is faithful." Sondra scraped the bottom of the jar and popped the last bite of banana into Emily's mouth. "It's in First Corinthians."

"Are you saying Chris is a temptation?"

Sondra laughed. "Not exactly. Chris is a wonderful Christian man. Just talk to him. You two can work something out."

Victoria stood and walked to the kitchen window. She believed with all her heart that God was faithful, and as far as Chris being a temptation went . . . well, she was tempted to run away from the Dukes of Hazzard look-alike and never acknowledge him again. But she couldn't do that. She had to face him, even if he sure seemed bent on loathing her. She peered outside and watched a hog wallow in the mud. She huffed. *Sure, Chris and I will work this out, when that pig grows wings and flies.*

CHAPTER 6

"Come here, Victoria. There's someone I'd like you to meet." Victoria scanned the crowded church lobby in the direction of Dylan's voice. She found him standing beside another man.

"Great," she mumbled between clenched teeth as she made her way toward them. "I hope he's not playing matchmaker."

"Victoria, this is Zack Bradshaw. He's one of the loan officers at our bank."

Victoria sucked in her breath. She needed to find a way to pay back Chris, but she wasn't ready to take out any loans. At this point, she didn't even have a job. Forcing a smile, she extended her hand. "It's a pleasure to meet you."

"The pleasure is mine. I hope this doesn't seem too forward. . . ."

Oh boy, here goes.

"Dylan was telling me that you're looking for a job. One of our tellers is going on permanent maternity leave." He laughed. "She'll *need* to stay home since she's having twins. But, anyway, I'd like to invite you to come by the bank and fill out an application."

Victoria could hardly believe what he said. A *job*. He was offering her a job.

"I have it on good authority" — the banker leaned closer — "that you'd have a good chance of getting the position, seeing as I do the hiring and Dylan's given you a gleaming recommendation."

Victoria stared up at Dylan, appreciating him more each moment she knew him. "Thanks, Dylan."

Glancing back at Zack, she took in his light blond hair sporting just the right length in a trendy hairstyle. His tailored gray suit spoke of the time he'd spent in the gym as well as being proof of his professional status. He wasn't an overly big man like Chris and Dylan. In truth, he was just the right size for her to drink in the light gray flecks shimmering in his pale blue eyes. Maybe a little matchmaking wouldn't be all that bad. She swallowed the excitement bubbling inside her and nodded. "I'll be by first thing in the morning."

"I'll be watching for you." He winked, and Victoria thought her heart would melt. The man couldn't have been much older than thirty, and who cared about an eight- or ten-year age difference anyway. She surely didn't. It had to mean something that his size and coloring fit the faceless groom she'd dreamed of so many times after watching her favorite fairy-tale shows as a young girl. She could almost hear birds chirping their approval in the background. Biting the inside of her lip to squelch a giggle, she shook her head. *I have got to get a grip.*

Maybe God had brought her to this small Oklahoma town. After all, He worked all things together for good for those who love Him. He could turn the bleakest situations into something beautiful. Maybe He wanted her to meet Zack Bradshaw. *And what a nice, solid name.*

She lowered her gaze. "Well, I'd better find Sondra and tell her the good news." She nodded and walked away on shaky legs toward the hall she hoped led to the nursery where she and Sondra had dropped off the children before Sunday school.

Looking down at her light blue slacks and matching slip-on, heeled shoes, she smirked. "My wardrobe is definitely more fitting for a woman who works at a bank instead of a ranch." Excitement mounted within her as she thought of what Sondra said about God giving her what *He* could handle. Victoria knew that God was handling everything.

"Abby" — Chris motioned for his sister to follow him down the church hall — "we need to have a talk." He stopped a little ways before the nursery and turned to face her. I-don't-care-what-you-want reeked from her posture and expression, and Chris squelched the desire to put her over his knee and paddle her. "You whispered with your friend all through church."

She huffed and crossed her arms in front of her chest. "Did not."

"I watched you, Abby. You did." He glowered at her old jeans with a hole in one knee and her long-sleeved, green T-shirt that she had cut holes in the bottom of each arm for her thumbs to fit through. A dark blue, tighter T-shirt had been pasted over that. Her hair, pulled back in that same weird band, had pointy brown wisps sticking straight up and out all around her head. She looked more like a person going to a rock concert or just stepping out of bed than someone who'd just come from God's sanctuary to worship. "Abby, I know you're already grounded for a month."

She snorted. "Yeah, big brother, so

whatcha gonna do now?"

He thought for a moment. What could he do now? He didn't have any experience raising children. Abby was only nine years younger than he, and they'd spent their lives bickering like siblings. He'd never been a caregiver type to her. Until last year. "Next week, you're sitting with me."

Her mouth dropped open. "You're kidding, right?"

Chris shook his head, feeling pretty good about the discipline he'd just thought up. The punishment should fit the crime. You talk in church; you don't get to sit by the person you talked with in church. Maybe he could do this parenting thing after all. "Not kidding. Next week you can sit with me, and if it goes well, I'll let you sit with your friend the week after that."

Abby smacked her hand to her hip. "This is a big joke. I can't wait until I'm eighteen, *Dad!*" She popped her hand up to cover her lips. "Oops, I forgot. My dad died. You're just my *brother!*" She stomped away from him.

Okay, so maybe I'm not going to be writing any child-rearing books at this point. He raked his hand through his hair and then scratched his jaw. "Abby, come back here."

She waved him off. "I'll be in the truck.

84

Silent. Like a good little girl."

"Having some trouble?"

Chris looked behind him and found Sondra holding PeeWee's hand with Emily firmly planted on her hip. Her purse and a baby bag hung haphazardly off her shoulder. "I think you're the one having some trouble. Let me take something." He reached for the bags, but instead she handed him the live, wiggling bundle. Emily cooed and grabbed at his hair.

"That kid loves to pull hair." Sondra flipped several wisps behind her shoulder. "I'm going to have to cut mine short if I don't get her broke of that and quick."

"It's just fascinating to her, that's all." Chris tickled under her chin. She giggled and blew slobber bubbles at him. He wrinkled his nose and wiped her mouth with her bib.

Sondra laughed. "She's already insolent, a complete handful. Must be the way of women, even from the very beginning."

Chris caught the teasing tone in Sondra's voice and looked at her. "Abby's going to be the death of me. I don't know how to parent her."

"I can see that." Sondra pushed Emily's slipping shoe back up onto her foot. Emily protested and tried to kick it off again but failed. "Abby needs a woman in her life."

Chris thought back to a time somewhere around ten years ago when Abby had sat on the floor in front of the couch while their mom brushed her hair. She would count each stroke and say that Abby's locks grew softer with every one. "The woman who should be doing this ran off a year ago."

"I know that's hard on you both." Sondra grabbed a pacifier from the baby bag when Emily started to fuss. Popping it into the baby's mouth, she asked, "Have you heard from your mom?"

"Not a word. Not even an idea if she's still alive."

"I am sorry, but maybe there is someone who could help Abby grow into a young lady. She's a good kid down deep. We both know she loves the Lord."

"Do we? Most times I don't see any proof of the Lord in Abby's life."

Sondra picked up Matt who had begun to get fidgety standing in the hall. "Think of what she's like when she's helped me at the group home. She loves to play with the children and the baby chicks." She hefted Matt higher on her hip. "Remember how good she was with Lizzie and Jake before Grace came home from her mission trip and took custody of them. Abby's just struggling right now."

Chris remembered a week before when he'd seen Abby reading her Bible late in the evening. She'd had the purity book her Sunday school teacher had purchased for the teenagers, as well. Later he'd noticed she'd scribbled several notes along the sides of one of the pages. Not wanting to invade her private thoughts, he closed the book and put it on the dresser in her room. Chris sighed. "I don't know who would be good for Abby. I don't even know who has the time. Sweet Mrs. Nielson has tried to reach out to her, but Abby wouldn't really open up."

"She doesn't seem to open up to me either." Sondra chuckled when Emily started to whine and rub her eyes. "It may have something to do with my constant interruptions." She set Matt back on the floor and took Emily from Chris's arms.

"Maybe we should pray about it."

"That's a wonderful idea." Chris watched as Sondra's eyes widened, and she nodded her head. "Or maybe God has already answered our prayers."

"Victoria."

Victoria looked up just before colliding into Chris. He grabbed her arm when her

87

heel slipped from beneath her. Once steady on her feet, she glanced up at Chris. "Sorry." Looking to her side, she saw Sondra standing beside her.

"How was church?" asked Sondra.

Victoria smiled. "It was terrific. The music was wonderful." She peeked up at Chris.

"Thanks," he said. "I've been waiting for weeks for Lawton's bookstore to get that sheet music in. It's one of my favorite songs on the radio."

"I could tell. It was as if angels sang directly from your lips. My spirit wanted to rise up and fly with the eagles in the song." She bit her lip. *What am I saying? I sound like a complete fool.* Heat warmed Victoria's cheeks, and she knew blotches would soon follow on her face and neck. She looked back at Sondra. "I mean . . ."

Sondra raised her eyebrows and grinned. "Well, how was Sunday school?"

Bless you, sweet sister-in-law, for the change in subject. "I felt an instant connection with the people in my class."

"We were glad to have you," said Chris.

Victoria forced herself to look up at him. "Thanks."

"We don't often have newcomers. Usually people leave us singles and join the marrieds." Chris laughed. "I'd be happy to introduce you to more people in the group."

"It would be wonderful for you to make more friends," added Sondra.

Chris crossed his arms in front of his chest. "That's right. One thing I've learned from Abby, girls love to chat with friends."

"Well, I did meet one new person today."

"You did?" Chris's eyebrows lifted in surprise. Something about his tone seemed to mock her. *What does he think, that I'm inept at meeting people in any way but crashing into their bumpers?* She brushed the thought away. *I'm just imagining things.*

"I think I have a job."

"A job?" Sondra and Chris asked in unison.

"Yep."

"That's great," said Sondra.

"Dylan introduced me to a man who works at your bank. Zack Bradshaw."

Chris's eyebrows furrowed. "Hmph."

Victoria scowled at him. Why the man, out of nowhere, determined to set her fury wheels to spinning was beyond her. She'd never met a person who infuriated her so completely. "He asked me to come by tomorrow and fill out an application." She smiled and looked back at Sondra.

Sondra hugged her with her free hand. "That's wonderful news. You've got to tell me all about it" — she bounced Emily as the child started to fuss — "as soon as we get home. I think I'm going to have to get these kids home. Nap time is calling."

"I'll help." Victoria reached for the bags.

"No, you stay here with Chris. He needs to talk to you, too."

Victoria frowned. She didn't know what Sondra was thinking. Victoria didn't need to stay with Chris. She needed to help Sondra, to be away from Chris.

"I think God may have answered our prayers before we had time to actually mouth them." Sondra winked and walked down the hall. Before she could take two steps, Dylan had appeared and scooped PeeWee into his arms.

"Makes sense."

Victoria peered at Chris, noting the sarcasm that dripped from his words. She shifted her weight, anxious to get to the van and head back to the ranch. Something about the oversized mechanic made her uncomfortable. Not that he hadn't always treated her as a respectable man should, he just made her feel different. And it had nothing to do with the car accident. "What makes sense? What are you talking about?"

"Zack Bradshaw."

"Zack?"

"He's definitely your type."

Victoria lifted her purse higher on her shoulder and straightened to her full height. "And how, Chris Ratliff, would you know my type?"

He huffed. "It's obvious."

"I don't know why Sondra wanted me to speak with you, but I'm sure it wasn't so we could argue. Because I have no desire —"

He lifted his hand to stop her. "I'm sorry. I had no right. Zack's a great guy." He leaned his head back and glanced at the ceiling. "I'm just tired, overwhelmed really. I can't seem to get a handle on her."

Chris stared down at Victoria whose expression exposed nothing short of confusion. Why he had felt the sudden yank of jealousy at her mention of Zack Bradshaw was a mystery to him. He liked and respected Zack, and Chris definitely didn't have any interest in Victoria.

Taking in her matching blue pants and jacket, the way her hair fell curly and full at her shoulders, and the sweet, soft scent that washed over him when she was near, Chris wondered if maybe he did. He shook his head, needing to remember the purpose of this conversation, and in truth, he felt confident Sondra had a good idea. *Now to convince Victoria.*

"What are you saying?" Victoria placed a manicured hand on her hip. She seemed none too happy to have been left with him.

Chris motioned for her to walk ahead of him. "Could we talk a minute?"

"Sure." She didn't budge.

"We could sit in the sanctuary." She still didn't move. He grinned. "Or we could stand right here and talk."

Victoria exhaled. "Look, if it's about the money for your car. I know I should have gotten with you before. I need to be honest. . . ."

He lifted his hand to stop her. "I wasn't going to ask you about the money for my car."

"You weren't?"

"You said you'd give it to me." He motioned to his hand. "As good as in my hand, remember?"

Her mouth twitched. "Okay, so what are we supposed to talk about?"

Chris cleared his throat. "Well, I have a younger sister. She's a teenager . . . and our mother has been gone for over a year." He loosened his tie. "She's gotten difficult for me to handle."

Victoria furrowed her brow. "Okay, I've heard as much. What are you asking?"

92

"Actually, Sondra was saying that she needs a female influence. Someone who could teach her manners, how to be a lady." Chris shoved both hands in his pants pockets and studied the floor. "She must think you'd be good for her."

Silence permeated the hall. Most of the congregation had left the building. Anxious for some kind of sound, Chris jingled the change in his pocket. The cool metal had a calming effect on him, feeling good between his fingers.

"What do you think?" Her gaze bore into him with intensity.

The clear sincerity reflected in Victoria's eyes attracted him in the most basic of ways. He couldn't deny his attraction for her. Any man with a pulse would be drawn to her. "I think you'd be a perfect influence."

Victoria smiled. "Then why don't you introduce me to her?"

"Let's go. She's in the truck."

Calm down. Victoria scurried to keep up with Chris's much wider stride. *I have no reason to be nervous. The man whose car I trashed just wants me to be a good influence on his wayward sister.* Victoria exhaled, blowing stray curls away from her eyes. *How did I get myself into this?*

Scanning the parking lot, she noticed few vehicles remained. Sondra and Dylan stood on each side of the van leaning into it, probably buckling both children into their car seats. She knew the kids had to be on the verge of a complete exhaustion meltdown, so she'd have to make this introduction quick. Looking ahead of her, she noticed the aged, dark green truck occupied by an obviously disgruntled teenager.

Chris gently touched her elbow in a way that felt protective. His breath kissed her ear as he whispered, "I apologize ahead of time for anything Abby may say to you."

"Don't worry." Victoria, swatted the air as a knot formed and tightened in her gut. The attraction she felt for Chris made no sense, and she had to fight it. She focused on the truck, and as they drew closer, Victoria noted Abby's arms were crossed in front of her chest. The teen's clamped lips formed a straight line, and her squinted eyes glared out the windshield and past them, as if she were staring at the church.

Somewhere inside Victoria a giggle formed. She coughed and willed herself to squelch it, but it wouldn't go away. Feeling it wiggle its way up to her lips, Victoria couldn't shake Abby's resemblance to a younger version of Granny from *The Beverly*

Hillbillies and the sour expressions she constantly wore.

"Are you okay?" Chris stopped just before the truck and peered at her.

Victoria nodded and then covered her mouth with her bulletin as another giggle escaped. She walked to Abby's door to avoid looking at Chris for fear she might burst into full-blown laughter. Victoria sneaked a peek at Abby, whose eyes squinted in defiance. The teen bit her bottom lip, and Victoria wondered if Abby had trouble holding her own giggles at bay. The expression proved too much, and Victoria laughed. Offering her hand through the rolled-down window, Victoria said, "I'm Victoria. You must be Abby."

Abby half smiled and nodded.

Victoria coughed and tried to clear her throat to settle down but couldn't shake the smile from her lips. "Look, I'll just be honest. I'm new here. In fact, I'm the gal who hit your brother's car."

"You're the Mary Ann Mangler?"

Victoria raised her eyebrows and glanced at Chris, who looked away from her but not before she noticed his face had turned bright crimson. "Yes, that's me. Well, your brother mentioned that you —"

"Dylan, did you say you need some help?

95

I'm coming!" Chris yelled toward the Wards' van. Dylan looked up, an expression of confusion on his face. He eyed Sondra and shrugged. Chris glanced back at Victoria. "I'll be right back."

That dirty rascal. Victoria shook her head. *He just ditched me.*

"Chris can't take the heat," said Abby.

Victoria glanced back at the teenager who smiled, exposing perfect, white teeth and eyes that sparkled in merriment. "Abby, you're a beautiful girl."

"Huh?" Abby's eyes widened, and she leaned back in her seat.

Victoria pulled down the visor. "Look at yourself. You're a natural beauty. When you smile, your whole face lights up."

Abby sneaked a quick peek. "You think so?"

Victoria nodded. "Definitely."

Abby exhaled and tapped her fingers on the dash. "Okay, fine. I'll be your project."

"What?" Victoria stepped back in surprise.

"But only if you promise not to boss me around. I hate it when Chris does that. I'm seventeen years old. I'm not a baby."

"No, you're not a baby."

Victoria thought for a moment, unsure how to respond. She didn't have any experience mentoring a teenager.

"That is why Chris brought you over here to meet me, right?" Abby's tone took on a sarcastic flare. "Because I need a good female role model."

The truth shall set you free. The scripture sang in Victoria's heart. If she intended to mentor Abby, she planned to be as honest and genuine as she could be. They'd have to learn from each other.

Victoria grinned. "Yes, you're right. Beautiful and smart."

Abby nodded, and Victoria realized the teen needed her to be honest and upfront with her. "Okay. You want to come over tomorrow evening? I'm grounded, so I'll be there."

For the first time since she'd arrived in Lasso, Victoria felt needed in a way that had nothing to do with herself. Sure, she'd felt needed by PeeWee and even Emily, which was something Victoria had always yearned for. But helping Abby gave Victoria a purpose. She could shower the teen with all she knew about makeup, clothes, manners, boys. . . . Okay, maybe Victoria could use a little help in that area, as her experience had been little to none. It didn't matter. Victoria could feel that God had given her a project . . . and a friend. "Absolutely."

CHAPTER 7

Sitting straight and proper as she had been taught in etiquette class, Victoria clasped her hands, resting them on top of her crossed legs. The white, tiny-flower print skirt and matching bright green summer top she wore spoke of a mixture of professionalism and femininity. She had been careful to apply extra foundation to ensure coverage of the freckles that made her appear young. Taking additional precaution, she swept her long curls into a tight clip allowing only a few ringlets to escape and frame her face.

Lord, please let me get this job. And let me get my Suburban back. She thought of Sondra taking a sleeping Emily from her bed and buckling her into the car seat. PeeWee had been happy to make the trip to Lawton, but Victoria knew it to be an unplanned excursion and interruption in a busy day for Sondra. *Hopefully I'll get my vehicle back soon.*

A middle-aged lady with a beehive hairdo approached Victoria. She held a stack of folders in her hand. Her frazzled expression bespoke that the last thing the woman wanted to do was take care of a job applicant. "Mr. Bradshaw will see you now."

"Thank you." Victoria rose and gripped her bag. She glided with ease in her nude-colored heels across the carpeted floor. If Victoria knew nothing else, she knew how to conduct herself as a lady in a public setting. She could thank her mother's determination that Victoria attend every one of her etiquette classes for that. Today she hoped the training would pay off.

Walking through the mahogany door, Victoria noted the soft contemporary Christian music playing from somewhere in the room. She smiled at Zack's greeting. His entire face seemed to shine, and his eyes smiled with his lips when he saw her. As a woman, Victoria sensed his approval of her appearance. Flutters of excitement and pleasure coursed through her at the realization.

"Have a seat." He motioned to the leather chair that sat across from his oversized, mahogany desk. Scanning the room, Victoria noticed wall-to-wall bookshelves, some adorned with popular Christian books she recognized as her own favorites.

Squeaks momentarily overpowered the music as he sat in the large matching leather chair behind the desk. Glancing at her potential employer, a paneled window streamed light from behind him, giving Zack an innocent, angelic appearance. His light, masculine scent filled her senses, and Victoria couldn't deny her attraction to him.

She lowered her lashes as she obeyed his bidding to sit. "Thank you."

"Victoria, you are more than qualified for this position." He glanced at her application. "You majored in business in college and seemed to do well. Did you have any positions in mind before coming to Lawton?"

"Not really."

"Your lack of an employment history probably does hurt your job search." He furrowed his brows. "You never had any part-time employment through school?"

She shook her head, realizing Zack must not know her history. *He must be fairly new to the community.* Everyone she spoke with, everywhere she went, seemed to know her as Sondra's sister-in-law. As she thought about it, that probably wasn't accurate. Most people recognized her as the Mary Ann Mangler, as Abby put it.

She smiled at the thought. The mishap

had given the townsfolk something to talk about, keeping them from thinking about her background. Maybe the wreck had been a blessing in disguise. She needed a fresh, new start. The last thing she wanted was for people to learn she was the daughter of an oil magnate who'd embezzled a large sum of money.

She remembered Chris's stunned expression when he saw the damage to his car. She thought of him jumping out of it to wipe bird droppings from the windshield, proof of how much the car meant to him. Chris would never think of the wreck as a blessing.

"What about transportation?" asked Zack. "Lasso's a bit of a drive from here."

"I should be fine. I hope to have my Suburban back very soon."

"Well, Dylan's recommendation covers any lack of experience you have, and I'm sure they'll help get you here until you get your vehicle." The young banker stood and extended his hand to her. "I'd be glad to offer you the position."

Victoria stood as well, almost wavering against the inviting scent of his cologne. She grabbed his hand, soft as her own, and realized Zack Bradshaw might just very well be the man she was looking for. "Thanks so much. When do I start?"

"Can you start training now?"

"Absolutely." Relief flooded over her. Finally, things were starting to look up.

Chris touched the back of his neck. Having just gotten a haircut, he could almost feel the hot shaving cream the barber lathered on the back of his neck before taking a straight razor to it. That was his favorite part. His neck felt soft as a peach with no fuzz.

He walked over to his truck and hopped inside. Scooping up his work ledger, he made sure he had recorded his business expenses and payments correctly. He'd been busier than usual this week and planned to spend some of the extra income on parts needed to fix Mary Ann.

Of course, Abby needed a few more pairs of jeans and a few long-sleeved shirts before school started in a little over a month, so he'd have to set a bit aside for that. He tallied a second time to be sure he'd made as much as he thought. Once finished, he leaned back against the seat and looked through the windshield up to the heavens. *God, You are so good. You promised to provide what we need, but already You have provided enough for me to get some of the parts I need to fix Mary Ann.*

Smiling, Chris grabbed the checks he needed to deposit and jumped out of the truck. He whistled "Amazing Grace" as he strode along the downtown sidewalk toward the bank. A contemporary version to the old hymn popped into his mind, and he shifted his tune, mentally playing the notes on his guitar. *I'll have to try it like that when I get home tonight.*

He opened the front door to the bank. An older lady who supported herself with a cane walked through. He nodded to her and waited for her to get through before he let the door shut behind him.

Looking up, he saw Victoria and Zack behind one of the teller booths. Victoria was sitting on a high-seated stool. Zack leaned over her shoulder and pointed to something on her desk. Something stirred inside Chris.

He watched as Victoria nodded, picked up a pen, and wrote something down. A sweet expression wrapped her face as she looked back up at Zack. A knot formed in Chris's throat, and his temperature rose when Zack smiled down at Victoria.

Chris could see the words "Good job" drip from Zack's lips, and then Victoria lowered her eyelashes and gazed back down at the paper. The muscles in Chris's arms began to twitch as anger raced down them. *What is the matter with me?* Chris glanced at the painting on his left and then shook his head and shoved his fists in his jeans pockets.

I'm full-blown jealous. He glanced at Victoria, who now sat alone in her booth. She seemed busy writing something on a notepad. The green shirt complemented her dark curls and light complexion. She looked like a breath of fresh summer air. But he couldn't be jealous over Victoria. The notion was ridiculous on too many levels.

Just get your deposit done and get on out of here. It's been a long week. He walked toward her and placed his checks and deposit slip on the counter. "Hi, Victoria."

She jumped. "Chris, I didn't hear anyone come in."

"I see you got the job."

"I did." She clasped her hands, and Chris couldn't help but notice how perfect her nails seemed, how soft her hands looked. He also noted her fingers were bare of any jewelry except a small silver band on her right-hand ring finger. She added, "And I love it already."

"That's great." All thoughts and words seemed to escape Chris. He stood looking at her, taking in that he'd never before noticed her lips actually had a kind of pouty shape to them. They were appealing and seemed to be more enticing with each blink.

She cleared her throat. "Did you want to make a deposit?"

"Yes." Chris pushed the checks and deposit slip closer to her.

"It may take me a minute." She smiled. "I'm new at this, you know."

"Take your time. I took the day off to run errands, get my hair cut, stuff like that."

She glanced up at him before turning back to her computer. "Your hair looks nice."

He felt his ears burn at her compliment. "Thanks."

She finished the transaction and handed him the receipt. "You were my first bank customer."

Chris noted the slip with the correct amount and account numbers typed on it. "Well, you did a great job."

"You know, I'm supposed to come by and spend time with Abby today, but I don't know if I will be able to."

"She'll understand that you had to work."

"It's not that. I get off at four, but I hate to ask Sondra to come pick me up, take me to your house, and then have to pick me up again." She sighed. "I'll be glad when I get my Suburban back."

"I'll be in town. Why don't you let me pick you up at four, and then I'll take you home whenever you're ready?"

Victoria peered at him. "Do you really want to do all that for the Mary Ann Mangler?"

"I'm beginning to see that the Mary Ann Mangler is a very nice woman who doesn't deserve that nickname."

Victoria's eyebrows rose. "Oh? And what nickname does she deserve?"

Chris felt his stomach knot and his chest tighten. He had to admit he was falling for her. Falling for her hard. Now he had to decide if he wanted to ignore his feelings or if he wanted to go after this girl. He cocked his head as nicknames of endearment and love filled his mind. "Fresh air," he whispered.

"What?"

He shook his head and willed his attraction to take a backseat in his brain. "Never mind. So will you come? Can I pick you up at four?"

"Sure. I'll call Sondra and tell her she doesn't have to worry about me." Victoria placed her hand on Chris's. His heart sped up with the touch, and he feared she could feel his racing heartbeat through his veins. "Thanks for trusting me with Abby."

Abby? Trusting her with Abby wasn't anything. It was the fact that she seemed to be taking hold of his heart that had him worried. "Think nothing of it."

Victoria pulled her favorite pink-grapefruit lipstick from her purse. She applied it to her lips and then smacked them together. Four o'clock had arrived quicker than she would have imagined. She rearranged the curls she'd allowed to frame her face. The clip in her hair had held tight, but she couldn't deny her longing to let her hair fall to her shoulders. She didn't know when she'd kept it up for so many hours.

After placing the lipstick back in her purse, she pouted at her reflection in the bathroom mirror. Zack had already left work for some type of meeting at another bank. Victoria had hoped to be able to talk with him more. She'd even come up with a few questions she could ask him intermittently through the day. She sighed. Her plan had been a sneaky one, and deep down she knew that wasn't pleasing to God.

I'm sorry, Lord. I don't know what to say to a man, especially one like Zack. But I don't want to be sinful or manipulative either.

Determined not to ask Zack a single phony question when she saw him the following day, Victoria walked out of the restroom and bank to see if Chris had arrived. She spied him waiting in the parking lot in his green truck. Walking over to him, she poked her head in the passenger's window. "Hey, thanks for picking me up."

"It's all right." He patted the seat. "Hop in."

She had to yank hard before the heavy door squeaked its willingness to let her do just that. Lifting one foot up to the floorboard, she grabbed the sides of her skirt and giggled. "I didn't know it was such a leap to get into this thing."

"There's a handle above your head."

"You're kidding." She looked up, and sure enough there it was. Victoria grabbed it with one hand and held her skirt with the other. With a quick hop, she pulled herself inside and slammed the protesting door.

"I didn't think about you needing a change of clothes," said Chris.

"What?"

"There's no telling what Abby will want you to do."

Victoria frowned. "Aren't I supposed to be the one influencing her?"

Chris laughed. "Yeah, and I hope you can do it. Just the same, you'd be more comfortable in jeans or shorts. Abby will probably have some you can wear."

"Okay." An uneasiness gnawed at Victoria. Surely she hadn't gotten in over her head with Abby. She leaned over and grabbed the handle to roll up the window. Having never seen one before except on television, Victoria wasn't sure exactly how to work it. The handle was stiff, but she turned it both ways until she managed to get the window to rise.

"No air-conditioning."

"What?" She gawked at Chris whose mouth split in a full grin.

"The truck doesn't have air-conditioning. You'll have to leave it down."

"Well, this should be an adventure."

"I'd reckon it will be." Chris turned the key in the ignition. It grumbled and then roared its willingness to start.

Bluegrass gospel music pealed from the radio as the inside of the cab shook like they were in the middle of an earthquake. Victoria felt as if she'd stepped out onto some newly remade *Twilight Zone* program. She grabbed for her seat belt only to have it fight her for several moments to stretch long enough to fasten into its lock.

Chris put the truck into DRIVE and pulled out into the street. Heat from the engine seemed to wrap around her feet making her start to perspire. She could feel wisps of hair slip away from her clip. Her shirt blew hard against her skin as the wind whipped all around her.

The cab jerked and bumped over every dip in the road. Her purse fell onto the floorboard, and she bent over to pick it up. As she sat up, Chris must have hit a pothole because she was popped high in the air. She gasped when her bottom reconnected with the torn, vinyl seat.

"You okay?" asked Chris.

Victoria had never felt like this. She'd never been in anything so primitive, so rustic, so nostalgic. *Okay, Victoria, you're being a little dramatic.* But she didn't care. She felt so country . . . so free. She loved it.

Grabbing her clip from her hair, she shook her curls loose and kicked off her heels. She glanced at Chris whose expression bespoke nothing short of complete awe. "This is great."

"Um . . . okay." Chris peered back out the windshield. Victoria couldn't help but notice his chiseled chin and how stubble, a much deeper red than his hair, covered it. Strong arms gripped the steering wheel, and she realized how protected she felt in Chris's presence.

She shook her head and glanced out the

passenger window. The wind blew the blanket of flat, golden wheat in ripples before her. She shouldn't think about Chris and his chin or arms or anything else for that matter. A country boy/mechanic obsessed with naming his inanimate treasures after women — no, Chris Ratliff could not be the man for her. He was nothing like Zack. And Zack was perfect.

CHAPTER 8

What have I gotten myself into? Chris watched as Victoria hopped out of the truck and held open the door. She giggled as she ran her fingers through the tousled curly mass that sat atop her head. Her wind-kissed cheeks matched the nail polish he'd inadvertently noticed covering her toenails.

Abby threw open the screen door. "Hey, Victoria." His little sister waved at the woman who'd stolen his breath the entire trip home to come inside. "What's so funny?" Abby asked as a smile split her much-too-dark-painted lips. The first smile he'd seen in days.

Victoria glanced back at Chris. "Your brother's truck."

Abby furrowed her brows. "What?"

"That truck is great." She scooped her heels from the floorboard and slammed the door shut.

"What's so great about it?"

"It's like an amusement park ride. It bounces and turns, jerks and twirls."

Chris shook his head as he stepped out of the cab. "The lady spent a long time stuck inside a bank today." He looked at Abby and circled his finger beside his temple. "Too many hours counting greenbacks, I guess."

With her heels dangling from her fingers, Victoria stomped around the truck toward him. She lifted her shoulders and peered up at him. "I'll have you know I had a great time on my first day of work."

A long strand of hair fell in front of one of her eyes while the mass of it hung down her back. Her tiny nostrils flared in a pitiful attempt at anger. Her eyes betrayed her as they sparkled with merriment.

He cleared his throat. "I'm glad you had a good day."

"You" — she poked the middle of his chest — "were my first customer." She smiled, and her face lit up brighter than the sun peeking through a batch of rain clouds.

He brushed the wayward strand away from her eye. His fingers caressed her soft cheek. "I'm glad I was your first customer."

Her face flushed, and she touched her cheek. Chris gripped the door handle as he fought a primitive urge to scoop her lithe

113

body into his arms and carry her off to a cave somewhere far away from civilization.

Instead he turned and grabbed his keys and the papers from his day's errands out of the truck. He shrugged at Abby as he walked toward the house. He looked back at the two. "Victoria doesn't have a change of clothes. Would you mind her borrowing something of yours that's a little more comfortable?"

"Sure." She glanced at Victoria. "You're a little taller than me, but I'll see what I can find."

"Let's go then." Victoria walked to the door. When she stood beside Abby, Victoria lightly bumped the teen with her hip. Abby giggled and grabbed Victoria's hand, dragging her fully into the house.

Chris shook his head and grinned. Sondra Ward had to be the most intelligent person he knew. Victoria would be the perfect person to influence Abby.

Victoria squelched the gasp that threatened to escape when she stepped past the mudroom and into Chris's kitchen. The furniture seemed to be in good condition, but the house was a wreck. Dishes, covered in every imaginable food, overflowed on one side of the double sink. Clean dishes had been stacked just as high on the other side. *Do they even have any dishes in the cabinets?* The stove had some sort of grime coating the top. Papers and notebooks, a purse, a pile of clothes, and even a lone tennis shoe sat on the counters and kitchen table.

"Sorry 'bout the mess," Abby said as she guided Victoria past the kitchen. "I have a bad habit of dropping everything at the door." Her teen friend looked back at her, and a glimmer of pain shot through Abby's expression. "Used to drive Mama crazy."

"Oh, I don't mind a bit."

And in truth, what did it matter that the kitchen was a little disheveled? That's what she had come for anyway . . . to show Abby how to be a lady. And Victoria knew that part of being a lady was learning how to pick up after yourself. In fact, she hadn't spent too many hours of her life cleaning dishes and clearing counters — okay, she had never done any kind of manual labor in the home. Still, she always picked up after herself, and she knew *how* to clean dishes and whatnot. Surely Victoria could help Abby get on the right track.

They walked through a surprisingly clean living area. At a quick glance, Victoria marveled at how comfortable the room felt. Dark furniture circled an oversized wood

115

fireplace. Various pictures of Chris and Abby adorned the walls. Victoria wanted to stop and look at their childhood memories, but she hurried after her protégée instead.

"Here we go," Abby said as she opened her bedroom door.

"Wow!" Victoria raised her eyebrows in surprise. Never in her life had she seen such a disaster. Tornadoes couldn't do so much damage. Clothes, wrappers, CDs, books, more items than Victoria could take in, were strewed all over the room.

Victoria shrieked, and her blood drained from her head and pooled in her feet when a small, yapping object leaped from atop a pile of clothes. Placing her hand on her chest, she willed her heart to slow down as Abby scooped the little fur ball into her arms and allowed the creature to lick her face.

"This is Sassy-Girl." She buried her face in the ball of hair. "She's my bestest buddy in the whole world." Turning to the animal, Abby's voice took on a high, childlike pitch. "Ain't you, baby? You're my precious wittle girl, ain't ya?"

The copper-colored animal yelped and wagged her tail wildly.

Swallowing, Victoria hesitantly reached toward the animal. Yaps sounded from the dog in continual succession, so Victoria gingerly lowered her hand, palm up, under the animal's nose. Sassy-Girl sniffed for several moments before her tail began to wag. She licked Victoria's palm, and Victoria had to conjure up all the effort she'd ever known not to hurl on the floor.

"She likes you." Abby squealed.

Victoria shrugged. "I guess so."

"No, you don't understand." Abby placed her hand on Victoria's shoulder. "Sassy-Girl doesn't like anyone. All my friends tease about her being the grumpiest dog they've ever seen. She doesn't even like Chris half the time."

"Hmm." Victoria cautiously reached for the dog. Sassy-Girl wagged her tail feverishly and practically leaped into Victoria's arms. "I've never had a dog, but I always wanted one." She held the animal in the crook of one arm and petted her with her free hand. "What kind of dog is she?"

"She's a Pomeranian. You can love on her any time you come over." Abby grabbed Sassy-Girl from Victoria's grasp and placed her back atop the pile of clothes on her floor. "But let's get you out of that snazzy outfit before she gets hair all over you." Abby shifted her weight from one side to the other and then crossed her arms in front of her chest. She bit the inside of her lip and twitched her mouth. "I don't think I have anything that will fit you."

Victoria took in the tiny frame of the teenager. The girl was a good four or five inches shorter than she, and though Victoria's size was on the slim side, Abby couldn't be considered anything bigger than petite.

"Hmm." Abby twirled a piece of her hair that was pulled up in a knot.

Victoria noticed how thick and lush the strand appeared. Her hair was long and dark and had potential to be stunningly beautiful. Why Abby had it tied in a ragged knot, Victoria didn't have a clue. That style, if worn too often, would do nothing but break her hair off in uneven pieces.

The makeup Abby wore was worse. The lipstick plastered on her lips smeared dark, too dark for Abby's light skin. Sure, dark-haired women often wore more bold lipsticks, but they were usually older and going to late-night events. On Abby, the color gave the impression of a girl who a law-abiding citizen wouldn't want to meet on the street when the sun went down. Her eyes were just as bad, covered in various shades of green. *Note to self: Be sure to explain to Abby that a gal should never wear eye shadow the same color as her eyes. It makes others focus on her makeup and not her natural beauty.*

Abby walked toward the bedroom door. "I'll be right back."

Victoria inhaled as she watched her young friend disappear down the hall. *And those jeans are atrocious. They do nothing to complement Abby's slim figure.* Yes, she had a lot of work ahead of her, but first things first. The two of them would need to go through the house and learn the fine art of picking up after oneself. Abby might just find she owned treasures she'd long forgotten about.

Abby walked back into the room holding a pair of sweatpants and a ragged Oklahoma State T-shirt. She lifted them up. "These are my brother's from years ago. They're too small for him now, so they may not be too awful big for you."

Victoria widened her eyes and pointed to her chest then toward the clothes. "You want me to wear those?"

Abby frowned. "If you don't mind."

Victoria forced her lips to smile. "Of course I don't mind."

Chapter 9

"Ready to go?" Chris handed Victoria her purse from the cleared table. The entire kitchen had undergone an amazing transformation since Victoria arrived some four hours before. The sun had finished its descent into the earth, and Chris knew Victoria had to be exhausted.

"Ready as ever." She held her heels in her hands. "Mind if I keep these off?"

"Would it matter?"

She shook her head and flashed him a smile that nearly knocked him out of his socks.

"Then I don't mind." He walked her to the truck and opened the door for her. Shutting it behind her, he went around the front and jumped into the cab. "I wondered if we could talk a bit?"

She gazed over at him. "About what?"

He shrugged. "About you. I figure if you're going to be spending a lot of time with Abby I oughta get to know you."

Her expression lit like a match. "You don't trust me?"

"I didn't say that."

"Not in so many words, but you implied it."

"No, I didn't."

"Yes, you did."

"Are you always this angry?"

"You make me angry."

Chris sighed. "Okay, I didn't mean to insult you."

"Then what did you mean?"

"I'd just like to get to know you, that's all."

"Make sure I'm not some kind of a masked murderer in disguise? You're the one who asked me to work with Abby."

He patted the top of the steering wheel and peered out at the star-filled sky. "Look, I didn't mean it the way it sounded. I'll tell you about myself. I've lived here all my life. Always wanted to work with cars. Always. Always loved to pick my guitar and sing for Jesus, too. I get to do that every Sunday at church. I'm pretty much doing what I always wanted."

He shifted his weight in the seat. "I didn't expect to finish raising Abby. Truth is, I'm not very good at it. I pray every day God will show me what to say, what to do, how to respond. Most days I end up flat on my face begging God to show me what to do with her."

Chris cleared his throat, fearing he'd been too honest with his shortcomings. He slowed down as a small rabbit jumped across the road and into the swaying wheat.

"It's great you've always known what you wanted." Victoria's voice was almost a whisper. "I graduated college and still didn't have a clue. No reason to. Daddy had lots of . . ." She laid her heels on the seat between them. "Well, anyway, I haven't really had any life goals. I accepted Jesus several years back, and since then I've just been trying to live each day for Him."

"Sounds like a good plan."

"It always has been, until . . ." She peered at him and smiled. "It still is a good plan. I really enjoyed spending time with your sister today. She's a great girl."

"I hope you're right."

"I am." She touched the top of his hand. "Thank you for trusting me."

CHAPTER 10

Placing her hand in the small of her back, Victoria sat up and leaned as far back as her body would allow. The sun had risen to its peak and beat down heavier on her and the garden. She wiped beads of sweat from her brow. *I don't think I've ever worked this hard in my life.*

Since it was a Saturday, Victoria had gotten off work at noon, and Sondra had dropped her off at Chris's so she could spend more time with Abby. She couldn't deny that cleaning the kitchen and Abby's room on her previous visit had been nothing short of a blast. Abby had a wonderful, sweet spirit and a quick sense of humor. Victoria didn't understand why Abby and Chris had so many battles.

"Uh, I think that was a plant." Abby pointed at the leafy object in Victoria's gloved hand.

Victoria furrowed her eyebrows. "I

thought it was poison ivy."

Abby covered her mouth with a dirt-caked hand. The black gunk had found a home beneath each of her fingernails as well as staining the creases of her fingers. Victoria frowned and wondered why the teen had insisted on attacking the garden bare-handed.

Abby giggled. "That's a green pepper plant."

"What?"

"You know. You can eat them raw or cut them up and cook them in meat loaf or chili. Some people even make stuffed green peppers."

Victoria swatted the air. "I know what they are. I just thought this looked like a poison ivy plant. Don't poison ivy stems have three pointy leaves?"

Abby nodded. "Yes, but that looks nothing like poison ivy. It's a green pepper plant." Abby smiled and pointed to the cushy-looking plant that Victoria had been unsure of what to do with. "You pulled the green pepper plant and left that?"

"I didn't know what to do with that. It looks so soft and fluffy. I thought it might be some sort of vegetation."

"It's a sticker weed."

"A sticker weed?"

"Yeah, at least that's what I call 'em. You know, it's real prickly like a porcupine."

"I suppose I should pull it."

Abby giggled again and nodded her head.

Embarrassed, Victoria grabbed the weed with all her strength and pulled. It didn't move. She was supposed to be the one teaching Abby about becoming a lady, and yet she was humiliating herself with her total ineptness at gardening. She yanked on the weed again. The thing seemed determined to stay in the ground, so Victoria pulled a little harder. It still didn't budge. *This thing has a mind of its own.* Grabbing one piece of it, Victoria yanked until some of it came up. She'd just have to get it a little at a time.

"I kept my room clean. Kitchen, too."

Victoria looked up. A strand of hair fell into her eyes, and she swiped it away with the back of her wrist. "That's great."

"Chris was real happy about it. Said if I could keep it up he'd give me more privileges."

"That's wonderful."

"Yeah." Abby pulled a small weed and threw it away from the garden. "But it's kinda weird, ya know. Chris and I have always acted like brother and sister, not like he's my dad. Sure, he's a lot older than me, but we used to play house together. He was

125

the dad, and I was the mom."

"Really?" Victoria raised her eyebrows in surprise.

Abby sat back on her bottom and chuckled. "I'd make him hold my babies and feed them and burp them."

Victoria laughed. "I can't imagine your big, burly brother so domesticated."

"Chris would do it until a friend came over or until he couldn't take it no more. Then we'd fight." She grinned at Victoria. "I mean, we'd really fight. We'd punch each other and roll around on the floor until Mama came and made us split up and go to our rooms."

"But he's so much bigger than you. He could have really hurt you."

"Well, that's the really funny thing. Chris was a scrawny little thing all through high school. It wasn't until after he graduated that he started growing."

"How interesting."

"Yeah, I could take him back then." Abby smiled. "Course, I don't think he ever put his real might into fighting me."

"I think he really cares a lot about you, Abby."

Abby grabbed up another weed and cast it away from the garden. "I don't know. He acts like my dad. But he ain't my dad."

"I know. He knows that, too."

"My dad was wonderful. He was perfect." Abby twirled a blade of grass between her fingers. "He used to come home from work and help Mama cook dinner. She would try to have it ready for him, but she never could quite get it done."

"Did your mom work, as well?"

"No. She had diabetes really bad, and she was always tired. She slept a lot." She paused. "After dinner, Dad, Chris, and I would do dishes. Every night. Chris washed. I dried. Dad put them away."

"Where was your mom?"

Abby looked at the grass in her hand. "Resting."

"Oh."

"Then Dad read Chris and me a Bible story. Every night." Abby paused. "I miss him so much."

"Abby, what happened to your mom?"

"She left."

"I'm . . . sorry."

Abby looked at Victoria. Her eyes filled with tears. "I don't know why she left us." She shrugged her shoulders. "I was angry for a long time, but now I just don't understand why she wouldn't listen to reason."

Victoria listened as Abby told her more stories about her parents and arguments she

127

had with Chris. Abby needed consistency, but she also yearned for compassion and patience in her life. Though her situation was different, Victoria understood all too well the teen's feelings of abandonment and confusion.

From what Victoria had seen of Chris, she could well imagine why the girl felt exasperated by her older brother. She herself had been a recipient of Chris's frustrated words or, at the very least, words said in such a way they came across as offensive. The man also formed unusual attachments to inanimate objects.

And yet she thought about him all the time.

She plucked another weed from the garden. How did Chris feel when all this happened? He must have struggled. Surely he needed to talk to someone. Maybe he had spoken with their pastor.

Still, Abby is his responsibility. He's already admitted the trouble he has relating to her. He has to see to more than just her physical needs.

Abby leaned over and wrapped her arms around Victoria. "Thank you for listening."

Victoria squeezed and then released Abby. "You're a wonderful young lady, Abby. You can talk to me anytime."

"Let's get this garden done so we can order some pizza."

"Sounds good to me." Victoria grabbed what she hoped to be a weed and pulled it out of the ground. *I think Chris and I need to have a little talk.*

Chris tapped the steering wheel to the tune of the music he planned to play at church the following morning. His day couldn't have been any longer — or any worse. Everything had gone wrong. He'd lost his favorite wrench, hit his head on the hood of a car, spilled a tub of old, nasty oil all over the garage floor, not to mention he never could determine what pained Mrs. Mitchell's car. He was booked full on Monday besides trying to squeeze in figuring out that car's ailment.

Inhaling, he pulled into his drive and looked over to find Victoria and Abby sitting in the garden pulling weeds. The memory of seeing Victoria just a few days before wearing his clothes filled his mind. Something in him had stirred in a way he had been unprepared for when he saw her small frame swallowed in his old shirt and pants.

He had pushed the unwelcome feeling away until that evening when he found the clothes folded on the corner of his bed. He picked them up to find her sweet scent had lingered, which forced his thoughts of her to whirl in his head like a tornado.

A tornado proved a perfect description for her. She'd come into his life, wrecked his pride and joy, and knocked him off his feet each time she came near. He couldn't eat without wondering what foods she liked. He couldn't receive money from his clients without seeing her behind the desk at the bank. He couldn't sleep without envisioning her long lashes against her cheek as he'd seen them that first day when she had prayed on the way to Sondra's farm. His whole life had gone topsy-turvy since Victoria Thankful slammed into it.

And there she was again with the sun shining down on her dark hair, setting reddish pieces in it afire with beauty. Abby adored her. Even Sassy-Girl loved her, which proved to be some weird miracle unto itself. That dog didn't even like him most of the time, and he usually fed her.

God, I don't know why she makes me feel this way. We both know she's not right for me. Rich versus poor — well, okay, working income. Beauty versus beast — well, okay, average.

What about Christian versus Christian, his

130

heart seemed to ask. He shook the thought away, parked the car, and got out. It didn't matter that they shared the same faith. They were direct opposites, and he'd like to spend his days with a wife with whom he had something in common. *Wife? Who said anything about a wife?*

In desperate need of getting the woman out of his mind, Chris was grateful when the time finally came to take her home. After opening the door for Victoria, Chris hopped into the front seat of his truck. "I appreciate all you're doing for Abby."

"She's a wonderful girl. I'm loving every minute of it."

"Good."

"Thanks for taking me home. I have court on Monday afternoon. Hopefully, after that, I'll have my Suburban back."

"That's great."

"I think on Tuesday, Abby and I are going to start working on how to wear hair and makeup."

Chris knew Abby needed all the help she could get in that area. "That would be wonderful."

Silence wrapped around them. Chris started to envision Mrs. Mitchell's car's engine. There had to be something he had missed, something he couldn't quite get a grasp of. Everything he'd checked looked good, seemed good. Mentally he removed each plug, trying to remember what he'd missed.

"Would it be all right if I took her to get her hair cut?"

Chris could hear Victoria's voice tense. He looked at her and frowned at the frustrated expression that overtook her face. Maybe he was just imagining things. It had probably been a pretty long day for her, as well. "That would be fine."

"She needs to feel accepted, Chris."

He glanced at her again. This time he could tell she was mad. "I agree."

"By you."

The words spit from her lips with what he was sure was vehemence. He tried to think of a time he may have made Victoria believe he didn't accept Abby and couldn't think of one. Abby seemed to enjoy making his life more difficult, but he loved and accepted her completely. "I do accept Abby."

"No, Chris, I don't think you do. This has been a very hard couple of years for her. She needs compassion and tenderness from you, not constant criticism and punishment."

"I don't think you know what you're talking about."

"Oh yes, I do. Abby told me you do little more than berate her. She said you are always looking for things to be upset with her about." She smacked her hand against her leg. "I have no trouble with Abby. She does everything I ask."

"You haven't asked her to do something she doesn't want to do."

"Oh yes, I have. Do you think she *wanted* to clean her room and the kitchen? And yet she did it, and she's kept both clean." She paused. "She's not used to you being her parent. She's used to you being her brother."

How dare Victoria criticize him for the way he treated Abby! How dare she be so condescending, so know-it-all with him! He did the best he could with his sister. Abby was the one who wouldn't give him a chance, who wouldn't listen to reason or a single thing he had to say.

Chris stopped the car in front of Dylan and Sondra's house. He willed the mounting fury to stay put in his gut as he turned to look Victoria in the face. Pointing to his chest, he said, "That's what I'm used to, as well."

Victoria flung the truck door open and jumped out. She leaned forward into the cab. "Then quit acting like such a jerk."

133

Slamming the door, she walked up the porch steps and into the house.

What was I thinking? I should have known Victoria Thankful would pull something like this. The woman lives to make me crazy.

He yanked the truck into gear and skidded out of the drive. Did Victoria take the time to ask him about anything Abby said? Did she give him the chance to tell his side? No! He was the bad guy. He was always the bad guy. Nothing he could do would ever be good, or even okay, in Victoria Thankful's eyes.

Well, what do I care anyway! I haven't liked that woman from the moment I saw her. He huffed and turned onto the road leading to his house. *And yet I can't seem to get her out of my mind.*

CHAPTER 11

Chris shut the hood of the car. Three
vehicles behind on his schedule, but he had
finally figured out what was wrong with
Mrs. Mitchell's car. Walking over to the
front desk, he called and left a message that
she could stop by and pick it up at any time.
He flipped through his appointment book
and growled. If he wanted to get through all
of them today, he'd have to stay until well
after dinner. Noting his filled calendar for
the rest of the week, he decided he'd order
a pizza and just go ahead and stay.

Dialing the number to his house, he
listened to rings and waited for the answering machine to pick up. Abby had gone to
the group home with Sondra to visit the
kids, so he needed to leave a message for
her so she wouldn't wonder where he was
this evening.

Abby's recorded voice sounded over the
phone. She sounded so young, so sweet. It

had been more than a year since Chris had thought of Abby and sweet at the same time. He remembered all Victoria had told him two days before. Did Abby really feel he didn't accept her? It had been hard for him to switch from brother to guardian. He still struggled with the reality, the truth of it. Of course Abby would struggle, as well.

He thought of Abby sitting beside Victoria during church. Both had smiled and clapped their hands while he played his new song. When the chorus came and he invited the congregation to join him, both seemed happy and ready to join in. In truth, he hadn't seen Abby that worshipful in over a year.

His mind replayed the rainy day that sent his already faltering world into a tailspin. "I can't take it anymore." His mother's voice sounded as plain as if she stood beside him.

He closed his eyes and saw her standing in the kitchen. Her eyelids were swollen over her dark eyes. Wrinkles spread across her much-too-quickly aging forehead. Graying hair pulled into a haphazard bun, she took a shaky hand and pushed stray strands behind her ear.

"I need some time." She grabbed Chris's arms with both her hands. She squeezed him tight, and he looked down and saw the suitcase at her feet. "I don't have the strength, the energy," she continued. Sobs wrenched her body, and she released him and shook violently. "I miss him so much."

"It's okay, Mama." Chris gazed past his mother and saw Abby standing in the kitchen door. Her eyes were swollen from crying, as well. "Chris and I will do whatever you need. We'll keep the house up and cook and whatever," she simpered.

"No!" His mother squealed back at Abby. She looked at Chris and shook her head. "No." Wiping her eyes with the back of her hand and sniffing, she leaned over and picked up the suitcase. She stood up straight and set her jaw. "I have to go."

Then she was gone.

Chris peered out the window of his shop. She'd said no good-bye. No "I love you." No "I'll come back soon." She'd simply walked out the door, and they hadn't heard from her since.

Abby had cried for days, but she didn't talk about it. He'd been thankful. He didn't think he could talk about it either. What could he say anyway? He had no answers, nothing that made sense. After his dad died, Chris had worked double the hours to make sure he provided for his mom and sister. Abby helped around the house, as she never had before. There were no logical reasons for his mom to walk out on them.

And yet she had.

Maybe he should have talked to Abby about it. Maybe both of them should have talked. Maybe he came down too hard on her. And the truth was, Victoria seemed to be filling a spot in Abby's life that had needed filling for quite some time. He never tried to be Abby's mom or dad, but maybe he hadn't been as open with her as he should have been.

God, show me how to reach my sister. Show me how to be a better brother. He thought of Victoria and the angry expression on her face when she slammed his truck door. He took a deep breath as he realized how much it hurt to have Victoria upset with him. *Show me how to make amends with Victoria, too.*

Victoria gazed up at the cold, stone structure. The courthouse's aged exterior didn't make her think of justice; it scared her. And why did every courthouse she'd ever seen look like some smaller version of the White House? She had probably read or heard the reason at some point in school, but she couldn't recall it. At the moment, she didn't care much about past history lessons. She wanted to get her vehicle back.

She opened her handbag and checked for the hundredth time to be sure proof of the six-month insurance plan was still inside. Sondra had already found out what Victoria's court cost would be, so she checked again to be sure she had enough for it. Looking through her wallet, she found her driver's license in its correct place, as well.

I'm as ready as I'm going to be. She inhaled and walked up the steps. After opening the heavy half-glass, half-wood door, she walked inside. Her heels clicked against the concrete floor, making the empty, enormous hall seem all the more overwhelming.

A door on her left had a sign that read CIRCUIT CLERK. To her right, she saw doors that read VEHICLE REGISTRATION and DRIVER'S LICENSE. *I don't think I'm supposed to go to any of those.* She grabbed the ticket Sheriff Troy had given her out of her bag. She was supposed to go to district court.

Scanning her left and right, she didn't see any doors that mentioned anything about a district court. Wishing she hadn't been so adamant with Sondra about not coming to allow PeeWee and Emily to take their naps, Victoria walked back to the front of the building where she spied a staircase with a sign that announced district and circuit

139

courts were held upstairs. She sighed in relief, gripped the handrail, and willed herself to scale the flight of stairs.

A few months ago, I would have never dreamed I'd be doing this. At that time, she'd been shopping in malls, spending any amount of money she chose on a pair of shoes or a perfect purse. She might have been out to lunch with her mother at the most expensive restaurants. Never would she have been going to court to get her Suburban back. She'd never even stepped foot in a courthouse.

God, I am absolutely terrified. Please let this go well. Let the judge be kind to me. Please let it be over quick.

It had been humiliating to have to take half a day off work for this when she'd been employed less than two months. Of course, Zack had been kind about it. In fact, he was kind about everything. Victoria still found herself drawn to him, and she felt certain he had almost asked her out on a couple of occasions; however, their conversations had been interrupted by an employee or a customer.

It was a mystery she didn't understand, but somehow she didn't quite feel a romantic connection with Zack. At first, she would have given anything to have him ask her out.

Zack had everything she'd ever dreamed of in a partner, and yet there didn't seem to be a spark between them. Yes, that was what she missed — the spark, that yearning-all-day-to-see-you-again feeling. Though she loved to see Zack, loved to talk with him, she just didn't seem to have the happily-ever-after feelings.

But then I've always been known to be a bit dramatic. Didn't Mother always say I lived in my own fairy-tale land all my life? She smiled at the remembrance of playing dress-up in her princess outfit as a girl. Kenny would begrudgingly pretend to be her prince.

I probably wouldn't know real love anyway. And doesn't the Bible tell us not to trust our emotions? Zack is perfect for me. A picture of Chris popped into her mind, and she shook her head. *I need to focus on getting my Suburban back.*

Reaching the top of the stairs, Victoria found the district courtroom and walked in. More people than she had anticipated sat in wooden benches facing the mound of wood the judge sat behind. Sliding into a pew beside an older woman and a small boy, Victoria looked around, surprised at the ornate features in the room. Flowers and loops and fancy shapes had been sculpted into the stone along the walls and ceiling. Three

141

enormous, antique chandeliers hung in a row from the middle of the ceiling. The room screamed of history, and Victoria found herself wondering about the people who had sat in her very seat years and years before her.

She gazed up at the man seated at the front, the judge she'd dreaded for several weeks. He did seem to be as gentle as a puppy. His face hung in wrinkles, reminding her of a bassett hound. Not a single hair topped his head, except the gray circle that wrapped around just above his ears. He looked like a grandpa, a cuddly, friendly grandpa.

"Betty, Bobby," the judge spoke to a young couple in a slow, soft voice, "I can't give you your van back."

"But Judge Henry, I haven't been able to get to work," the man responded.

The judge shook his head. "Bobby, I spoke with your pa last night. He said he'd been offering you rides and you wouldn't take them."

"But . . ."

"No buts. You can't have your vehicle back until you have insurance. That's the law."

"Judge . . ."

"Now listen, son." Judge Henry leaned forward. Concern wrapped his features.

"You two have yourselves a little one now. It's time to grow up, Bobby."

"I am grown." Bobby puffed out his chest.

"Then take care of your family. It's time, Bobby." The judge leaned back. "Tell you what I'll do. Seeing how I've known you since you were toddling around the court-house steps, you come back in two weeks. If you've gone to work every day, I'll even sport you half of what you need for three months' worth of insurance."

"Thank you, Judge Henry." Betty smiled. "I'll see he gets to work every day."

Bobby grumbled but didn't say anything else as he followed Betty out of the court-room. Victoria leaned back in the pew. *I think Chris was right. The judge seems like a very kind man.* She watched as Judge Henry dealt with a few more cases before hers. Finally, her name was called.

Standing, she felt the ease slip from her body as her stomach twisted with nervous-ness. Her heels clicked louder than ever as she made her way toward the front. The judge peered down at his paper and then at her. "Victoria Thankful, I presume."

Her voice squeaked. "Yes, sir."

A slow smile formed on his lips. "No need to be nervous, dear. I'm Judge Henry. It's a pleasure to meet you."

She nodded and willed her hands and legs not to shake.

The judge leaned back in his chair. "So you're the Mary Ann Mutilator."

"I thought it was Mangler."

Judge Henry laughed and smacked the top of the podium. "I think I've heard it both ways. So have you made arrangements with Chris yet?"

Dread filled her stomach. "Not yet, sir."

"No need to worry. He didn't press any charges, and he's a good man. He'll give you time."

She nodded, praying the judge would hurry. She felt the stares of everyone in the courtroom. Swallowing, she feared she might lose her breakfast at any moment.

"Do you have your license and proof of insurance?"

"Yes, sir." She took the papers from her purse and handed them to him.

He read through her insurance papers and frowned. "You didn't have insurance at the time of the accident."

"No, sir. My" — she cleared her throat — "my insurance policy had run out, and I wasn't aware of it."

"Hmm." He shuffled through the papers again and then glanced up at her. "Technically, I can cite you for not having insurance at the time of the wreck, but since Chris didn't press charges and you made arrangements to get insurance so quickly, I'll let it go."

Relief flooded her heart. "Thank you so much, sir."

"You will have court fees."

"Yes, I know."

He handed the papers back to her. "Well, young lady, I think I'll send you on your way. You can pay your fees downstairs and walk next door to the sheriff's office to get the keys to your vehicle."

"Thank you, sir."

"You have a good day, Ms. Victoria Thankful."

"Victoria Thankful?" A male voice sounded from the back of the room. "Are you Victoria Thankful, the daughter of Thomas Thankful?"

Victoria peered at the back of the room. Her feet seemed to freeze beneath her as she didn't recognize the man.

"Well," he continued, "are you the daughter of the man whose business name was Marcus George?" He walked toward her. "The man who was an oil magnate caught embezzling money?"

"Young fellow, what are you talking about?" asked Judge Henry.

145

"Your Honor, I'm just wondering if Thomas Thankful is her father."

Victoria's heels nearly fell out from beneath her. She grabbed the nearest pew and looked away from her accuser. The gazes of more than twenty people glowered at her. Most seemed confused. A few had already recognized the name and seemed downright angry.

"Well, I . . ."

"Are you?" The black-haired man's face would have been handsome except for the expression of contempt that wrapped his features. "My cousin was supporting his wife and four children on the income he made from working at a Thomas Thankful's oil company. When the man was found to be embezzling money and decided to evade the law and run off to who-knows-where, my cousin lost his job. And now he's about to lose his home."

Judge Henry hit the podium with his gavel. "That's enough. Victoria is not on trial about her father, in any way, shape, or form."

Tears filled Victoria's eyes. She had been devastated by her father's actions and so consumed with her own dilemmas because of them that she hadn't really considered the families who had been affected by her father's misdeeds.

"He has a daughter." The man had reached her side. He whispered, "Are you her?"

A tear spilled down Victoria's cheek, and she peered at the ground. "I am."

With all the energy she could muster, she fled amid the murmurings of everyone in the room. Running down the stairs, she composed herself and made her way to the correct office to pay her fee. No one followed her. *They're probably all discussing the many ways Daddy hurt families they knew. God, how could I have been so selfish not to think of the pain he'd caused others?*

Swallowing back her imminent spilling of emotion, she made her way to the sheriff's office, got her keys, and found her Suburban. With the turn of the ignition, the dam of her heart broke and tears spilled from her eyes. How much devastation had her father caused? Pain for that family, pain for other families, and pain for her own life seemed to stab at her insides. *Why, God? Why did Daddy do this?*

CHAPTER 12

"Hi, Abby." Chris walked into the kitchen to find Abby sitting at the kitchen table peeling potatoes. His sister's transformation had been amazing since Victoria started visiting. She hadn't gotten her hair cut as yet, but Victoria had taught Abby how to wear her face paint a coat or two lighter. Chris had forgotten that his little sister's lips were actually pink in color and not some funky dark shade of purple.

"Hey, big brother." Abby half smiled, but her voice sounded distraught. "Have you seen the paper?"

He shook his head and opened the refrigerator. After grabbing a water bottle and an apple, he sat down at the table across from his sister and picked up the weekly newspaper. "Anything happen this week?"

Abby huffed. "You could say that."

Chris frowned. It must have been pretty big news to capture Abby's attention. The girl only flipped through the pages to find the TV guide. He started to skim the front page. *An accident on the other side of town with injuries. Another water advisory notice and some town council suggestions on what to do about its continual reoccurrences.*

"Look at the bottom," said Abby.

Chris opened the page to its full length. He almost choked on his apple when he saw a picture of Victoria leaving the courthouse. The caption above it read, "EMBEZZLER AMONG US?"

"It's Victoria," said Abby. Chris looked up to see his sister's eyes pooled with tears. She placed the potato peeler on the table and swiped her eyes with the back of her hand. "You and I both know she's not an embezzler."

Chris tried to skim through the article, but as tears raced down Abby's cheeks, he lowered the paper and touched the top of her hand.

"She doesn't even have the money to pay you for Mary Ann. She's not a criminal." Abby pulled a tissue from her jeans pocket and wiped her nose.

"What does it say exactly?"

"Remember that guy they showed on all the stations who'd taken money from his oil companies?"

Chris thought back to the news stories a few months ago about an oil magnate who had embezzled money from his company, but that guy's name wasn't Thankful. *What was that guy's name? It was George, somebody George.* "But that's not her dad," said Chris. "That man's last name was George."

Abby shook her head. "No, George was his business name." She stood and walked toward the bathroom. "I don't know what's going to happen. I'm afraid Victoria will want to leave." She covered her face with her hands. "I need her here." She ran into the bathroom, slamming the door behind her.

Chris's heart pounded with uncertainty. Maybe he should try to talk to Abby. But what would he say? He didn't even know what was going on. Besides, he didn't know how to talk to Abby. That had been their problem since long before Mom left. He glanced at the bathroom door where Sassy-Girl had already made her appearance. She pawed at the door just as Chris heard the water running in the shower.

Sighing, he picked up the paper and read through the article. *This can't be right.* He scratched his chin and read through it once more. He rolled up the paper and stuck it under his arm. *There's only one way to find out the truth of all this.* Grabbing his keys, he walked to the bathroom door. "I'll be back, Abby. Go ahead and fix supper. I'll find out what's going on."

The door opened. A towel was wrapped around Abby's head, and a much-too-big robe hung from her small frame. Her face had been scrubbed clean and shiny, but her eyes were still red and swollen. She didn't say anything; she just sighed deeply and then looked up at him. Her expression begged him to make it all better.

An urge he hadn't had in months filled him. Without thinking, he grabbed Abby into a tight hug. Sobs overtook her, and she cried into his shoulder. He combed her hair with his fingers and held her tight. She drove him crazy, but God had blessed him with his little sister. God had also given him the job of taking care of her. With Victoria's help, he now realized that meant providing more than food and clothes. Sometimes it meant a hug, a compliment, a promise. "It's going to be all right. I'm not letting her go anywhere."

Abby peered up at him. "Promise?"

He closed his eyes, overwhelmed with a mixture of feelings. Loss for his dad. Loss for his mom. A real need not to lose Victoria. Suddenly he understood how much all of it felt to Abby, too. "I'll do my best."

His mind spun in a whirl as he drove to the Wards' ranch. Was Victoria a fraud like her father? The reports about Mr. George's dealings with employees and business partners had been appalling. He thought of how upset Victoria had been when he'd given her his estimates to fix Mary Ann. In his gut, he knew she had been genuine in her want to make amends for the accident.

After pulling into the driveway, he yanked the keys out of the ignition and scaled the steps up the porch. Before he had time to knock, Sondra opened the door. Her lips parted in a smile that didn't quite make it to her eyes.

"Where is she?" Chris asked.

"At the bank." Sondra motioned for Chris to come inside. "I just laid the kids down. We can talk."

Chris followed her into the house. The sweet smell of fresh-cut roses filled his nostrils as he walked into her kitchen and saw a vase full sitting on her table. Dylan leaned against the counter taking a swig from his coffee mug. Upon seeing Chris, Dylan put the cup down and offered his hand. "Good to see you."

Chris barely shook it before he took the paper from under his arm and opened it.

"What's this about? Is it true?"

"It's true."

"But Victoria. What does that mean about Victoria? Is she a fraud? Has she been lying to us since she got here?"

Dylan crossed his arms in front of his chest while Sondra sat at the table. She looked up at Chris. He could tell her gaze searched him at the depths of his being. "What do you think, Chris? You've been around Victoria. Do you think she's a fraud?"

Chris frowned. Sondra's words were not said in accusation or malice. They were formed — stated exactly and perfectly. She was asking him to decide within himself what he knew to be true.

His mind played reels of moments he'd spent with Victoria. He drifted to the day he found Abby and Victoria working in the garden. He thought of the time she had deposited his money at the bank. He saw her with PeeWee in her arms the first time she'd met the little guy. "No. She's not a fraud." With the words spoken aloud, Chris knew without reservation they were true. "What did happen?"

"Mama, I no feel good."

Chris glanced toward the hall just as Pee-Wee vomited all over the floor. Sondra

153

hopped up and ran to him as Dylan grabbed paper towels from the cabinet. Scooping up the boy, Sondra raced to the sink as another bout of sickness came. Chris looked over to find Dylan gagging as he wiped up the mess from the floor.

Emily started to cry from her bedroom just as Chris's cell phone began to vibrate in his coveralls pocket. Dylan picked up the drenched paper towels and carried them to the trash. The smell must have overwhelmed him, because once he reached the can, he was sick. Ignoring his phone, Chris turned toward Sondra who had already stripped PeeWee down to his birthday suit. "You want me to check on Emily?"

Hacking sounded from the baby's bedroom, and Sondra looked at Chris, her eyes big as the headlights of his car. "No. You better run. We must have the stomach virus that's going around." Sondra exhaled and grabbed a two-liter bottle of lemon-lime soda from the cabinet.

Chris's cell phone began to vibrate once more. "You sure? I can stay and help. What do I do?" His stomach clenched at the idea of cleaning vomit, but he'd do it to help.

Dylan tore a clean paper towel off the roll and wiped his mouth. "Sondra's right. You get on out of here so you don't get sick, as well."

Chris grabbed his cell phone from his pocket as he walked toward the front door. He looked back at Dylan. "If it gets to be too much, you call me."

"Vic." Sondra turned from washing her hands at the kitchen sink. "Can you pick up Vic? Wouldn't you know the poor woman gets her Suburban back, and my van breaks down! I dropped her off at work."

"Not a problem. I'll get her. Do you need me to look at your van?"

"I think it's something I can fix." Dylan smiled as PeeWee streaked buck naked across the floor yelling for his mom to help his sissy. "You run on out of here. Your day's a'coming."

"I don't know about that." Chris laughed as he opened and then shut the front door behind him. He flipped open his still vibrating phone. "Hello."

"Mr. Ratliff?"

"Yes."

"This is Vern from the pawnshop."

"Yes?"

The man cleared his throat. "Well, it's been well over a month since that gal brought that pretty little ring to my shop. I tried giving her a bit of extra time, but I'm

155

planning on putting that little beauty on my shelf today. I promised you I'd call first."

Chris's mind churned with a sudden idea. The more he thought about it, the more he liked it. "Yes, I'd like to purchase it. How much do you want?"

The man quoted the price he had told Victoria she'd have to pay to get it back. Chris's heart sank. It would take every penny he'd tried to save to get the right bumper for Mary Ann. A slow smile formed on his lips. *Vic's worth every penny.* "I'll be there in half an hour."

"Victoria, I'm going to be honest with you. I'm in a bit of a quandary."

She looked at the man standing behind his desk. Once again the light streaming from the window behind him wrapped his frame, giving him an almost angelic appearance. This time his expression held anything but pleasure.

Zack gripped the back of his oversized leather chair. "I've spent the entire morning on the phone with my boss, as well as several presidents from our sister banks."

Victoria leaned her head back and closed her eyes. Overwhelming anger and frustration filled her to her core. She'd had nothing to do with her father's embezzlement;

she'd barely even been to his office. Sadness washed over her with urgency. People would always associate her with "the embezzler." She choked back her yearning to scream, to cry at the unfairness of it all. *God, give me the patience and self-control to make it through this meeting with Zack without outbursts of any kind.*

She looked around the room. How many times had she dreamed of being back in this office with Zack gently touching her hand and asking her to accompany him on a romantic evening of a candlelit dinner and a quiet walk in the park? Or maybe he would ask her to a movie and an ice cream afterward.

She gazed at the man who fit her every dream for the perfect mate. Not this. Never in her daydreams of Zack Bradshaw had she imagined this.

"I want you to know I believe in you, Victoria." He moved from behind his desk until he stood just inches from her. "You and your father are not the same person."

Victoria glanced at her shoes. Her perfect, pointy-toed, brand-name, crème-colored shoes. "No. No, we're not."

"My hands are tied, though." Zack squeezed her shoulder as if to reassure her. "I have to put you on suspension until your father's investigation is over."

Gazing into his eyes, Victoria could see it pained Zack to do this. He had fought for her. He didn't have to say it. She could see the truth in his eyes. "I understand."

And she did. How could she blame a company — a bank, to be exact — for feeling uncomfortable letting the daughter of a multimillion-dollar embezzler work there until she had been cleared of any wrongdoing? "It's okay, Zack."

She turned to leave his office. Her mind swirled with problems. She had planned to buy back her grandma's ring. Now she couldn't. She had insurance to cover her Suburban for a few months, but now she wouldn't have gas money to drive it around. And Chris. How would she ever pay him to fix his Corvette?

"Victoria." Zack grabbed her hand. She turned and looked at him. His gaze held a yearning she had longed for weeks to see. "I really care about you. I've been praying and pondering how to ask you. . . . I mean, it's a little awkward because you're an employee. . . . I mean, there aren't any rules or anything; I just haven't been sure how to approach you. . . ."

Victoria watched as Zack fumbled with his words. Words she had waited for. Words she had played and replayed in many different ways in her mind. His beautiful, blond hair lay in a perfect style crowning his head. His eyes glimmered with a mixture of regret and want. His clothes had been pressed to perfection and hung perfectly on his formed frame. His hand, soft as her own, covered hers.

And she felt nothing.

How could she feel nothing? Zack Bradshaw was the epitome of the man she wanted, the man she needed. But she didn't want him. She didn't need him. The truth of it hit her with such force she couldn't deny it. "Zack, you're my friend."

He tightened his hold on her hand. "Please, Victoria. If it's about your job, believe me, I know you're an honest person. I trust you with every account in this bank."

She shook her head. "I believe you, Zack. And I believe you're my friend, as well." She smiled when the words left her lips.

He let go of her hand and nodded. Exhaling, he said, "I'm glad we're friends."

"I'll see you at church on Sunday," she said as she walked out the office door.

"Yes, Sunday."

Walking out the front door of the bank, Victoria saw Chris's truck parked across the street. "Hey." She recognized the voice and the large figure that loomed beside her.

Glancing up at Chris, her heart flipped, and she was surprised at how glad she felt to see him. "Let me guess. You're here to pick me up."

Chris laughed. "Seems the kids start puking their guts out when I come around."

"You do have that effect on people."

"Thanks."

"Seriously, are they okay?"

"Yeah, Dylan and Sondra have it under control." Chris shoved his hands in his pockets. "But I'd like to talk to you if you wouldn't mind."

"About the paper?"

He nodded.

"Sure, why not? It's not like I haven't talked about it enough today." Victoria smacked her hand to her thigh and then gazed up at Chris and realized he was exactly who she wanted to talk to.

CHAPTER 13

"Do you mind if we run by my shop a sec?" Chris jingled the keys in his hand. "I'm supposed to deliver eggs tomorrow, and the truck I use for my By His Hand ministry is in desperate need of some new plugs."

Victoria watched as a slight breeze danced through his hair. His need of another trim belied subtle hints of the wavy thickness that rested upon Chris's head. Being late in the day, stubble covered his jaw and chin, and Victoria wanted to feel the contrast between the two. "Without a ride, I'm at your mercy."

Chris frowned. "My truck can wait. I wanted to talk to you, too."

"I was just kidding. I didn't mean to sound snippy."

"Been a long day at work, huh?"

"You could say that." She lifted her purse higher on her shoulder and started toward Chris's truck. "But it's the last one, for a while anyway."

"What do you mean by that?" Chris came up beside her.

"It seems I'm on suspension until my dad's case is decided." She turned and looked at him. "I'm assuming you've read the paper."

He nodded. "That's why I want to talk, remember?"

"Yeah."

"But I don't understand why Zack would suspend you. It's hardly your fault."

Victoria noticed the anger that laced his words and realized that Chris had taken her side. Not that there really were sides to take, but it felt nice to know he didn't believe her to be a thief. She touched Chris's rough hand, so unlike any she had ever touched. It felt strong and stable, a blue-collar worker's hand, and she liked it. "It wasn't Zack's fault either. His boss made him, and I'm really okay with it." She released his hand and grabbed the handle to the truck door. "Except that I don't know how I'll pay you . . . or get back my grandma's ring," she mumbled as she hopped into the truck's cab.

Chris pushed the door shut behind her. "Don't you worry about paying me. I should be paying you for all the time you've spent putting up with Abby."

Victoria peered down at her manicured fingernails, the very ones she'd spent hours scrubbing garden dirt out from under after Abby convinced her to feel the earth between her fingers. She thought of how humiliated Abby must be to know the woman who's teaching her to be a lady has a criminal for a daddy. "I love your sister."

"She loves you, too."

"Has she read the paper?"

"Yes."

"What does she think of me now?"

"She made me promise to make you stay in Lasso."

Victoria looked into Chris's eyes. "She did?"

The honesty in his gaze nearly took her breath away as he nodded. His Adam's apple bobbed as he swallowed slowly. The yearning in his expression made her afraid to ask if he wanted her to stay, as well.

Her emotions consumed her. Maybe it was just plain exhaustion. Tears filled her eyes and spilled down her cheeks in such a race she had no chance to make them stop.

As she tried to swallow back her cries, Chris scooted over in the seat and wrapped his arms around her. She leaned into the crook of his neck, inhaling the deep scent of him. Without realizing it, her senses had come to recognize the smell of Chris Ratliff — his smell, the one that made up the man. She loved the scent and found comfort in it. She nestled her face into his shoulder. He tightened his hold, and she'd never felt so safe, so secure.

"It's all right, honey," he crooned and gently raked his fingers through the length of her hair.

"I don't want to be embarrassed anymore. Why doesn't God rescue me? What purpose is there in torturing me?"

"Oh, Victoria." Chris loosened his hold and lifted her chin toward him. "You listen to me. God loves you. He has a plan for every season of your life. He'll take care of you during this time." He caressed the side of her cheek. "Maybe He'll use me to help."

Victoria gazed at Chris's lips. She felt his desire to kiss her. Closing her eyes, she admitted how much she wanted it, too. She leaned toward him and allowed their lips to meet. His stubble scratched around her mouth, but she didn't care.

He tightened his embrace. "Promise you'll stay." He gazed into her eyes, and she knew he sought permission to kiss her again. Without reservation, she closed her eyes and found his lips once more. Without a doubt,

God had sent her to Chris.

I love her, Lord. Chris peered out the windshield at the buildings lining Main Street. He flipped his turn signal on and turned toward his shop. Glancing at Victoria, he tried to read her silence. Was she angry with him? Maybe he should apologize for kissing her, and yet not even a morsel of remorse filled him over those kisses. Everything in him longed to kiss her again.

He turned off the truck and opened the door. Before he could get to her side, she had already hopped out. He looked down at her, and she smiled and blushed. *I don't think she's angry with me.*

"I'll try to fix it as quickly as I can." Chris guided her inside. He showed her the refrigerator, the snacks, and the magazines, and then he escaped to the back of the shop. He popped the hood of the truck and removed and replaced the old plugs as quickly as possible.

He stood to his full height, glanced at the clock on the wall, and realized Sondra and Dylan might be worried about Victoria's whereabouts. Leaning over the truck, he made sure all the caps were tight. "You might want to call Sondra and tell her where you are," he hollered so that she could hear

165

him in the other room.

"I already called her."

Chris bumped his head on the hood when her voice sounded from right behind him. "Ouch." He rubbed the top of his head.

She placed her hand over her mouth and giggled. "Sorry about that."

"How long have you been standing there?"

"Awhile." She leaned against one of his tables. "Did you know you hum church hymns while you work?"

He felt the heat rush up his face. "Guess I hadn't thought about it."

"It's nice."

Chris walked over to the sink and washed his hands with detergent to get the grease off. He turned and looked at Victoria. She was more than he'd ever dreamed of, in every way. After drying his hands, he walked to her and touched her cheek. "You're beautiful, Victoria."

She smiled and walked toward the door. "I'll wait for you in your truck."

Victoria laid her Bible and prayer journal on her bed and her cookies and milk on the nightstand. She flipped on the lamp and then nestled into her covers. She thought of Chris standing next to the truck in his shop, in his element. Grease stains covered his legs and hips, not to mention his hands and arms. He even had the cutest smudge across his forehead. *And the kiss.* Victoria had never felt such a connection in her life. Even now she tingled all the way to her toes with the memory of it.

God, guide my feelings for him. They're so strong. Please tell me if they're from You. She took a bite of a cookie and then opened her Bible to Ecclesiastes. Since she'd accepted the Lord into her life, she'd been reading a chapter of the Bible each day. God never ceased to amaze her at how He spoke to her through His Word no matter where in the Bible she was reading.

She started at chapter three, her heart open and ready to accept whatever God showed her, especially concerning Chris Ratliff. After taking a drink of milk, she almost choked when she read verse one. She read it again. "There is a time for everything, and a season for every activity under heaven."

"God," — she peered up at the ceiling — "what was it that Chris said to me today?" She thought about when she'd cried into Chris's neck and shoulder. She'd asked him why God would allow all this to happen to her. *What did Chris say? It was something about You being in control of every season of my life.*

She shut her Bible and closed her eyes. "God, what Daddy did has been so hard, but You are in charge of everything in my life. You can use anything for Your glory. Anything."

She thought of Chris saying that maybe God would use him to help her. A shiver of excitement ran through her at the remembrance of his words. "God, I would have never asked this when I first came to Lasso, Oklahoma." She bit her lip and grinned as she mentally looked up at the overgrown mechanic. "But if You want to use Chris to help me, I'm okay with that."

CHAPTER 14

"Is that what it's supposed to look like?" Chris cupped his jaw, willing himself not to cover his eyes at the exposure of his sister.

He had agreed to take her shopping for a dress for her advanced chorus concert. Mrs. Smith had given the girls two requirements for attire. The dress needed to be semiformal, and it had to be black.

"I think most of the girls will wear one like it." She lifted one of the spaghetti straps higher onto her shoulder. The straps continued down her back in crisscross fashion, exposing skin to her waistline. Cut off in a flair at her knees, the length wasn't too bad, and the front of the dress appeared modest enough. But the back . . . He shook his head. "I don't know if I like this one, Abby."

"Oh, come on, Chris." Abby pouted.

God, Abby and I are having a good day, but I can't let her wear that to the concert. Chris cleared his throat and sat back in the chair.

"Hmm. Well, how do you feel about it? Does it feel a little more revealing than you'd have wanted?"

She twisted and touched her waistline as she gazed into the three-way mirror. "Maybe a little." She spun around, allowing the bottom to twirl. "But I love the skirt part."

The clerk tapped her index finger to her lips. "I think we have another one that's similar but isn't backless."

Abby smiled, and Chris exhaled. "Let's see it," they said in unison, and Abby giggled.

An hour later, they left the department store with a much more modest dress and matching heels. He watched as Abby hopped into the cab of the truck. Her eyes shone like a freshly polished grill on a new car. Thankfulness filled his spirit. He hopped into the driver's seat. "I'm glad we found something you like."

She clasped her hands. "Me, too. I had so much fun with you today."

"I had a pretty good time myself."

Abby half smiled. "You're not so bad after all."

Chris grunted. "Thanks." He started the truck and then sneaked a peek at Abby. She opened the shoe box to look at her purchase once more. "How 'bout we go to that

Mexican restaurant you love for dinner?"

Abby shut the lid. "You mean it?"

"Sure."

"I say this day can't get much better."

Chris knocked on the screen door at the Wards' ranch. "I brought your milk." He smiled when Victoria opened the door holding a sleeping Emily against her chest.

"You want to come in?"

"I probably should get the eggs and go."

PeeWee ran to the door with a cape tied around his neck. "Hi, Cis. I'm Sup–Man."

He raced away with his arms spread like an airplane.

"Where's Sondra and Dylan?" asked Chris.

"I told them to go for an afternoon picnic. They don't get much alone time."

Chris peeked inside and watched as Pee-Wee jumped from his toy chest to the floor then zoomed down the hall. "Better get the big one."

Victoria groaned. "Come on in." She walked over to PeeWee. "You can be Superman as long as you stay on the ground."

PeeWee nodded. "O–tay, Aunt Vic."

Victoria shook her head and looked at the ceiling. She glanced at Chris. "I'm going to lay her down, and then we can visit."

"Can I watch?" *Where did that come from?* He'd never been interested in babies and children. Sure, he liked them just fine, figured he'd even have one or two someday, but he didn't go out of his way to hang around them. Still, something stirred inside him when he saw Victoria holding baby Emily to her chest.

"Sure."

He followed her to the baby's room and watched as Victoria laid Emily in her bed. She petted Emily's hair and smiled. "She looks so peaceful."

Chris gazed at Victoria's profile. He drank his fill of her flowing curls, her light skin, her smooth neck. "You'll make a great mother."

Victoria looked up at him. "I hope so. I never thought about it before I came here. I've always been a fairy-tale kind of girl, dreaming of my Prince Charming."

"Prince Charming?"

Victoria looked up at him and smiled. "Yeah."

"You'd make a beautiful princess, Victoria, inside and out." He moved toward her, yearning to kiss her once more.

A crash sounded from the living room, and Victoria raced from the room. Chris grunted and walked out, as well. *If only the*

172

little guy could have waited ten seconds longer.

Victoria's hands grew moist as she walked toward the familiar building. It had been two weeks since the newspaper article, and she needed to pick up her last check from the bank. Trying to avoid as many coworkers as possible, Victoria had decided to go on Saturday. *Lord, please don't let Zack be here.*

Guilt filled her heart. Zack had been nothing but kind to her when they saw each other at church services. He hadn't done anything to make her feel as though he didn't trust her, and yet the thought of seeing him at the bank made her stomach queasy.

Her hand slipped from perspiration when she grabbed the long, metal door handle. *How embarrassing. Mom would die to know I'd let my nervousness show so much on the outside.* Grabbing the handle more firmly, she straightened her shoulders and pulled open the door.

"Hi, Victoria." Zack's smiling face greeted her from just inside the door. "Here to pick up your check?"

A thud landed in her gut, and she swallowed the pride mixed with embarrassment that threatened to heat up her cheeks. She forced herself to smile. "Yes."

"I'll get it for you." He escaped to the back office and then returned with her check in his hand.

"Can I go ahead and cash it?"

"Absolutely." Zack walked behind the counter. He grabbed a pen from beside the computer and handed it to Victoria.

Willing her hand not to shake, Victoria focused on writing her signature. She pushed the check toward him. "Thank you."

Zack opened a drawer and counted out her earnings. He then repeated the procedure as he placed the crisp bills in her hand. When he placed the last bill on top, he looked up at her. "Victoria, I'll be so glad when that case is over. Everyone is anxious to get you back."

Victoria looked up and into his eyes. He obviously meant every word he said. She gazed around the office. One of her coworkers waved from behind her desk. Victoria smiled and waved back. Putting aside her pride, she admitted how much she had enjoyed working at the bank, and it wasn't because of Zack at all. She liked all her coworkers, and she loved handing customers the cash from their well-earned checks and crunching numbers to be sure her drawer balanced correctly. She did want to return to her job. "I'll be glad, as well."

He touched the side of her hand. "Would you like to go to lunch today?" She looked back at Zack. "As a friend," he added, but his gaze told her he wanted to go as more than that.

She smiled. "Maybe another time. I'm heading out to Chris's house."

"Chris's?"

She felt her cheeks warm. "Well, I go out there to spend time with Abby."

Zack's eyebrows lifted, and he nodded slowly. "Abby's a wonderful girl." He exhaled a long breath and then winked. "Chris is a pretty nice guy, as well."

"Hey, Sassy-Girl." Victoria bent down and scooped the dog off the floor. Though she'd never had animals while growing up, she'd found them to be real treasures. Abby's dog always made her feel welcome and didn't care a whit about who her dad was and what he'd done. She lifted Sassy-Girl to her chest and allowed her to lick her cheek once. Petting the dog's head, she walked through the mudroom and into the kitchen. "Abby, you home?"

"In here."

Abby's muffled voice sounded from the

back of the house, probably Abby's room. When a sniff sounded, Victoria knew Abby had been crying. Victoria swallowed the lump in her throat. Though she and Abby had talked about Victoria's dad and the article in the paper, Victoria carried a deep fear that kids at school would make fun of Abby for associating with the "embezzler's daughter." Especially since the article came out just a few weeks after Abby had started her senior year.

Most of the townspeople received Victoria as they had before, probably because of Victoria's relation to Sondra as well as her consistent attendance at church, but still a few would yell cruel things to her from the grocery parking lot or mumble ugly comments under their breath at the gas station. Victoria remained determined not to let those people make her feel bad; she also knew the town had come to associate her with the Wards and the Ratliffs, and she surely didn't want to make things hard for any of them.

Victoria peeked into Abby's room to find her young friend sitting on her bed hugging her pillow to her chest. She sniffed and wiped the back of her hand across her eyes. Victoria set Sassy-Girl on the floor, and the dog hopped onto the bed and curled up beside Abby. Victoria's heart constricted. "What's the matter?"

Abby shrugged.

"Not ready to talk about it?" Victoria sat on the edge of the bed, allowing a little space between them.

Abby clutched her pillow to her chest. "It's Austin."

"Austin?" Victoria's mind raced through the people she and Abby had talked about since Abby had gone back to school. "Is that the boy in your advanced chorus class?"

Abby nodded.

If Victoria remembered correctly, he was the one with the striking blue eyes and sleek black hair who also played tight end for the football team. Victoria also thought he'd sounded a little too flirty and quite a bit too pushy for her liking. "What about him?"

"He asked me to the chorus dinner." Abby broke out into fresh sobs.

Victoria's mind raced. *What is a chorus dinner?* She'd been a bit of an introvert in school, but she had always known the usual teenage outings. A chorus dinner she'd never heard of. "That's okay. You don't have to go with him."

Abby smacked the pillow to the bed. "I want to go with him."

Victoria frowned and tried to think of

where the pain in this scenario was for Abby. "Okay then, I don't know what you're supposed to wear exactly, but it sounds fancy, so we'll find a gorgeous dress, and we'll fix your hair and makeup."

Abby shook her head. "I already have a dress. Chris and I went shopping, and he already agreed to let me get my hair and makeup fixed. My friends and I were going to go to Cut and Dried together the day of the concert."

Victoria felt a bit confused and had to admit the prick of hurt that stabbed her heart as to why Abby hadn't told her about the dinner. She would have loved to help Abby pick out dresses and hairstyles; however, this new piece of information was something to ponder. Abby had shared this special occasion with her brother, the very one who had known precious little of what to do with Abby when Victoria met him, who carried a handkerchief in his pocket and wiped bird droppings off his windshield with it, who often carried a wrench in his side pocket. And he, Chris Ratliff, had taken Abby shopping for a dinner dress.

A smile formed on Victoria's lips when she thought of the tough, burly man sitting in front of the dressing room's three-way mirror waiting for Abby to show him yet one more fancy gown.

"We were going to surprise you," Abby interrupted Victoria's thoughts.

"Huh?"

"Yeah. Chris and I wanted to show you how well we had done together." Abby shrugged. "Kinda show you how much you'd taught me."

"Oh, Abby." Victoria's heart felt it would burst with love for the young lady sitting beside her. She wrapped her arms around Abby and hugged her tight. "I am so proud of you . . . and Chris. It sounds like you're going to have a great time."

Abby pushed away and shook her head. "Nope. He dumped me."

"What?"

"Two weeks before the dinner, and Austin up and decides he wants to take Mallory instead."

"Oh, honey." Victoria grabbed Abby into a hug. "I'm so sorry."

"I don't even know why. He didn't give me a reason. Just broke off the date."

Victoria lifted Abby's chin. "I know just what we need. Go wash your face and get your shoes on."

Abby gasped. "I'm not going anywhere like this."

Victoria swatted her hand. "This is no

179

time to think about appearances. We have to do some seriously productive mourning."

Abby wrinkled her nose. "What?"

"We're heading to the store to splurge on every flavor ice cream we can find, and then we're going to stop by the video store and rent every funny movie we walk past. Then you and I will come back here and drown ourselves in icy sugar and ridiculous laughter."

One side of Abby's lips tilted up slightly.

"Come on now." Victoria stood and helped Abby up, as well. "We'll even share with Sassy-Girl."

The dog barked and wagged her tail. Abby wiped her eyes and headed toward the bathroom. "Okay."

Victoria counted the money in her purse. *Good thing I cashed my check.* Victoria sighed, knowing she should be cautious with the last of her income. She had planned to seek God in how to best spend and save what little bit she had for this indefinite amount of time. Splurging on ice cream and movie rentals probably was not the wisest choice.

Water spewed from the faucet in the bathroom, and then a cabinet shut. "Victoria." Abby peeked around the side of the door.

"Yeah."

"I'm so glad you came by today."

Victoria smiled as her whole being filled with a true sense of belonging. *Thank You, Lord. You never fail to guide me, even when it comes to how to spend the last bit of my earnings.*

CHAPTER 15

A flash of thrill filled Chris as he pulled up to the house and saw Victoria's Suburban in the drive. It had been a productive day at the shop; he'd even squeezed in an hour to work on Mary Ann between his afternoon appointments. But it had been a long one, as well, and seeing Victoria's beautiful smile and sparkling eyes would be the perfect reprieve from his work. He turned off the truck and hopped out.

Whistling, he bounded up the steps and opened the door. "Hello, Vic and Abby," he called as he kicked off his boots in the mudroom. The only greeting was laughter sounding from the living area. Turning the corner, he walked into the kitchen and found steaks marinating in some kind of good-smelling sauce. Toothpicks stuck out from every angle of the steaks — he assumed to hold in place the bacon that wrapped around each of them.

A squeal of laughter sounded again from the living room. He smiled as he walked toward them. "Sounds like we're having a good . . ."

He stopped when he reached the room. No less than ten partially eaten cartons of ice cream sat on the coffee table, the end tables, and the cushions of the couch. Abby sat on the floor with her legs crossed and three cartons sitting around her. Victoria sat on the couch with her knees under her chin and her arms wrapped around her calves. He couldn't tell if she was comfortable or possibly willing away a stomachache.

Once again Victoria sported an old pair of his sweats and shirt while Abby wore an old pair of pajamas. Both of them had their hair pulled up in a knot with strands sticking out from every angle. Chris wondered if the plan had backfired and Abby had taken the lady out of Victoria.

A noise sounded from the television, and both Abby and Victoria broke out into new peals of laughter. Chris glanced at the screen then back at the girls. Victoria stuck her spoon in a carton of chocolate-looking ice cream then licked the spoon. She glanced toward Chris. As her eyes bulged and her cheeks flushed crimson, he knew she'd just realized he'd gotten home.

He lifted his eyebrows. "Having fun?"

She uncurled her legs and hopped off the couch. "I didn't know you were here." She gawked at her watch. "Wow, it's later than I thought."

Abby looked up at him and waved. "Hey, Chris. We're in mourning."

"What?" Chris furrowed his eyebrows.

Victoria grabbed his hand and guided him into the kitchen. A stirring whipped through him as he followed the ruffled woman wearing his clothes. Maybe it was the softness of her skin or the light tickling of her fingernails when she touched him. Or maybe it was the wisps of hair that clung to the back of her neck from beneath her knot.

Whatever it was, he wanted to twirl Victoria around and grab her in his arms. He wanted to pull the knot from her hair and let the length fall down her back. He shook his head to clear his mind.

The time was coming when he planned to tell Victoria exactly how he felt, but it wouldn't be tonight in front of his little sister. Victoria stopped and whirled around. She rested her finger over her lips, telling him to be quiet. Leaning closer to him, her soft perfume filled the air. "Austin broke off their dinner date."

"What?"

"She's been really upset because he broke off their date, so we spent the . . ."

Chris walked away, opened the cabinet, and grabbed the church directory. "I'll take care of this. No boy is going to treat my little sister with such disrespect. He knows better than to do a girl like that." He flipped open the book.

Victoria put her hand on top of it. "Chris, don't. It will only make things harder for Abby."

Chris shook his head. "Austin knows better."

Victoria nodded. "Yes, he does, but if you call and his parents make him take her, Abby will be miserable. She'll resent you all over again." Victoria nudged him with her shoulder and grinned like a Cheshire cat. "I heard you took her shopping for her dress. I'm so impressed."

Chris bit his lip. Victoria's playfulness was about to undo him. If she wasn't careful, he'd be wrapping his arms around her and planting a firm kiss on her inviting lips. He looked into her eyes and shrugged. "It wasn't *too* bad."

Victoria stood on tiptoes and kissed his lips. "I'm really proud of you."

She didn't know what had come over her.

185

Chris just seemed so rugged, so manly with the blots of grease on his forehead and cheek. When his work-worn hands grabbed the directory with an urgency to right the wrong that had been done to his sister, Victoria nearly came unglued. She wanted him to care for her in such a protective way.

Actually, she wanted to talk to Chris about her feelings for him. They hadn't spoken of their kiss in the truck, and Victoria wondered if Chris had felt as much a connection as she had. She opened the refrigerator door and grabbed the ingredients for the salad. Shutting the door with her hip, she looked around the kitchen. Was she willing to live in this small country home?

The thought struck her hard as she placed the lettuce in the sink to wash it off. When Victoria insisted that Abby watch the rest of the movie, Chris had offered to help her cook dinner as soon as he cleaned up. The shower turned off, and Victoria knew it would be a matter of moments before he returned.

Her heart pounded as she considered a life of cooking every day. Sure, she had loved her time at the ranch. She had enjoyed collecting eggs, feeding chickens, cooking, and doing chores, but was she ready for the permanence of it? Maybe she had to be.

Daddy had taken the only life she'd ever known. She knew when he and Mother ran off her life would be different forever, so why did she suddenly feel burdened standing in Chris's kitchen?

"It smells wonderful in here." Chris walked up beside her. "What are you cooking?"

"It's my old cook's version of filet mignon. It's a little different than what you'd get in a restaurant. She used a light marinating sauce that softens the meat."

Chris rubbed his stomach. "Sounds good to me. I've never tried it, so I wouldn't know the difference anyway."

Never had filet mignon? Hadn't everyone had filet mignon? In Victoria's opinion, it was the best cut of steak. Additional proof their lives had been so different.

"What can I do?" Chris interrupted her thoughts.

"You can chop up the cucumber for the salad." She placed the knife and washed vegetable into his work-worn palm. She loved the strength in his hands. Surely she'd never resent their roughness or that they were permanently darkened from his work.

She gazed up at him. He towered over her even when he slumped to cut the vegetable that seemed so small in his grip. She loved his height, the mass of his shoulders and arms. His blond, reddish hair curled slightly at the nape of his neck. She wanted to touch the curl.

"All done. What now? The pepper?" He pushed the cucumbers to the side of the cutting board and grabbed the bell pepper beside the sink.

"Sure." She watched as he focused on his new task. No man who had ever been in her daddy's acquaintance would have stood beside her at the kitchen counter cutting vegetables for a salad.

She opened the oven to take out the potatoes. As she reached for the oven mitt, Chris grabbed it first. She contemplated him, and he smiled. "I'll get that for you." She watched as he lifted them out of the oven.

Remembering him standing before the church with his guitar in hand, flutters filled her heart. His love for the Lord proved undeniable. His kindness for her and his sister also attracted her in ways that every woman wanted. An inner excitement filled her as she admitted that if she got to spend every day for the rest of her life in this kitchen with this man, she'd savor every one of them.

Chapter 16

Chris lifted his guitar from its case and stood before the church to lead the congregation in praise songs. Looking out into the crowd, he saw Victoria seated in the second row beside Abby and one of her friends. He had already experienced enough pain in life to know how to praise God in the valleys. A smile tugged at his lips. Now he was learning to praise God on the mountaintops.

He raised his hands. "Stand up and praise the Lord with me." The people stood, and he started to pluck his guitar and lead them in worship.

His heart filled with awe for the Lord as words of love and adoration spilled from the lips of his brothers and sisters in Christ. He looked out and saw Grace and Eric Nichols who had married less than a year before and were taking care of Lizzie and Jake. Unknown to their congregation for several years, Eric had struggled with his past, but God had overcome all their trials.

He glanced at Sondra and Dylan, holding hands as they sang. God had given Sondra a second chance at love and Dylan a wonderful wife. He almost chuckled aloud at the thought of the many Wards he presumed he'd see running around the church building in a few years' time. He saw Mr. and Mrs. Nielson who still attended church every Sunday despite Mr. Nielson's battle with cancer and Mrs. Nielson's arthritis. Even when they had to prematurely turn the furniture business they loved over to their young son, the couple still remained faithful to the Lord.

His gaze traveled to Victoria. With her eyes closed and her face uplifted, he could tell she sang the praises from the depths of her spirit. His heart tightened. A few months ago, he had begged God to rid him of women. *I praise You, Lord, for answering that prayer with a No.*

"Victoria."

Victoria turned at the sound of Zack's call from behind her. He motioned for her to wait, so she moved away from the exiting congregation and toward a wall. Once he reached her, she smiled. "Hey, Zack."

"Hi. How have you been?"

"Good. And you?"

"Good. We're still missing you at the bank."

Victoria stared at her feet. "Yeah, I miss it, too. I hope my dad's case is settled soon. I'd really like to come back."

"Do you think it will be much longer?"

Victoria shrugged. "As far as I know, no one has heard from my parents. I don't even know where they are."

"I'm sorry about that." Zack shoved one hand in his pants pocket and adjusted his tie with the other. "Victoria, we are friends, right?"

Victoria gazed at him. "Yes. I think so. What's wrong?"

"Well, I have a favor to ask you." He pulled at his collar. Victoria noticed a spot of perspiration on his forehead.

"Zack, what is it?"

He leaned closer to her. "I really don't want anyone to know."

Her curiosity piqued and a giggle formed in her throat at the secretive expression on his face. "Okay."

"I'm trying out for Lawton's community play."

"I didn't know you liked to act." Victoria studied Zack, feeling perplexed at the crush she'd had on him when she'd really known nothing about him.

"Well, it's kind of a closet passion. I've always been interested but too shy to try out."

"Why now?"

Zack stared past her, and Victoria turned to see what he was looking at. A young redhead came out of the ladies' restroom. Her short, springy curls bounced when she walked. She gazed at Zack with ice-blue eyes and then smiled for the briefest of moments.

Victoria chuckled. "Rosa?"

"Shh." Zack put his fingers to her lips. "She's trying out, as well. Look, I've got the script, and I just don't want to fall on my face. I hoped you might rehearse with me."

"You know it's a musical."

"Yes. It's a production of *Oklahoma*."

"That means singing."

"I know."

Victoria lightly punched his arm. "Zack, I didn't know you sang."

"Well, I can't sing as well as Chris, if that's what you're getting at, but hopefully, I'll be able to carry a tune well enough. So will you help me or not?"

Victoria covered her mouth to squelch her laughter. "Of course I will. I'm so happy for you." She gave Zack a quick hug. "So when do you want to meet?"

Chris felt as if someone had punched him in the gut. He had been sure Victoria felt the connection he did. Preparing dinner with her the week before had only confirmed his feelings. Now she was hugging Zack and promising to meet him. *What a fool you are, Ratliff.*

He grabbed the keys from his pocket. Clutching his Bible tighter in his hand, he determined to walk past them without their noticing. Abby came up beside him and touched his arm. "So did you ask her?"

"No." He walked toward the door, willing Abby to take his lead.

"Don't be nervous, Chris. I know she'll say yes."

"I don't intend to ask . . ."

"Victoria!" Abby yelled as she grabbed Chris's arm tighter. With her free hand, she motioned for Victoria to come to them.

Great. Now what do I do? Victoria's whole face lit up with a smile as she walked toward them. "No, Abby. Don't say anything."

Abby grabbed her hands when Victoria reached them. "Guess what? I'm going to the chorus dinner with Tyler."

Victoria's eyes widened, and Chris couldn't help but smile at Victoria's genuine interest in his sister. "You didn't tell me before church."

"I thought Chris was going to tell you."

"Chris?" Victoria frowned and peered over at him.

"Yeah. The school needs chaperones for the dinner, and they asked Chris, and he was going to ask you to go with him." Abby jumped up and down and clapped her hands. "It'll be so much fun."

Victoria gazed up at him. The intensity in her eyes nearly took his breath away. "You were going to ask me to her dinner?"

"Well . . ."

"I think he thought you'd say no, but I told him you wouldn't. I don't know what these guys worry about."

Chris wanted the floor to open up and suck him down into the center of the earth. Humiliation washed over him until he felt sure his entire body had turned the deepest crimson possible.

He exhaled and watched Victoria. She bit her bottom lip, and he could see she was about to laugh. She nodded. "I'd love to go."

CHAPTER 17

Chris knocked on the Wards' front door. Sondra opened it and smiled. "Hey, Chris."

"Hey. Here's your milk." He handed her two quarts. "I came by to pick up the eggs for By His Hand."

"They were beside the barn, weren't they?"

"Yeah." Chris shoved his hands in his pockets. "I wanted to remind Vic about the dinner tonight, also."

Sondra smiled. "I think she remembers. She had the most beautiful dress dry-cleaned."

Heat warmed his cheeks. He felt like a young high school kid standing on his girl's porch waiting for approval from her parents to come inside. "Well, I was going to make sure she knew I'd be by at six."

Sondra bit her bottom lip, but not before a little giggle escaped. She placed her hand on her hip. "You want to talk to her yourself?"

Chris wanted to growl. He didn't know why Sondra seemed bent on making this so hard. Yes, he wanted to talk with Victoria. The last time he'd spoken with her, she'd been talking about meeting up with Zack.

He wanted to mention the dinner and then gauge her response to see if she just felt sorry for him on behalf of Abby. He could have put his little sister over his knee for the way she practically shamed Victoria into going to the dinner with him, like he was some kind of pity case. Well, he had news for the both of them: He could get a date if he wanted one. He wasn't sure whom he'd get a date with, but he knew he could find one.

"She's around back." Sondra chuckled and then bit her bottom lip a second time. "I'm sure she'd love to see you."

Chris mumbled a thanks under his breath and then strode around the house. He didn't know what Sondra found so funny. Maybe it was the thought of Victoria and him as a couple. Who was he kidding? Sondra was right. They were as opposite as night and day, as oil and water, as Ford and Chevy.

He rounded the corner and saw Victoria

leaning all the way over in a patio chair painting her toenails. A blue robe swallowed her, and numerous small curlers stuck out all over her head. She sat up, and her eyes bulged, surrounded by a goopy green mess of gunk that covered her face and neck. "Chris!"

"Hey." A slow smile lifted his lips.

"What are you doing here?" She dropped the nail polish, tightened the robe around her chest, and turned away from him, all in one swift movement.

He laughed then. "I came by to pick up eggs and thought I'd remind you that I'd be here at six tonight for Abby's dinner."

She didn't look at him. "I remembered."

"Good." He eyed her toes and realized the nail polish had fallen and spilled on the patio. "Oops. The nail polish fell." He bent down to pick it up.

Victoria turned and leaned over, as well. His head met hers, and some of the goopy green stuff smashed into his forehead. "Sorry," she squealed and sat up and away from him.

"What is this stuff anyway?" He wiped some off his forehead and smelled it. It had a clean, yet medicinal kind of odor.

"Chris, you're not supposed to see a lady like this."

"Like what?"

Victoria huffed and turned back toward him. She waved her hands up and down. "Like this. I'm getting ready for the dinner." She crossed her arms in front of her chest. "You're not supposed to know it takes" — she crossed her legs — "it takes this much effort to get fixed up."

She turned away from him again. Chris held back his chuckle at her exaggerated dramatics. He didn't want her to be embarrassed. "Okay. I'll leave, but I'll be back at six."

"Okay." She didn't look at him. Chris could hear the uncertainty in her tone.

"Victoria."

"Yes?"

"Look at me."

He waited as she sighed and then slowly turned toward him. Taking her hand in his, he rubbed his coarse thumb against its softness. "You could go in a potato sack, and you'd still be the most beautiful person there."

She contemplated him for a brief moment, and then she smiled. "Thank you, Chris. I'll see you tonight."

Victoria clasped the strand of pearls around her wrist. Her grandmother's ring would

have been a beautiful accent to the matching necklace and bracelet set that Sondra
had loaned her. She looked at her naked
finger. But she'd never have the opportunity
to wear the ring again. When she'd called
the pawnshop owner a little over a month
after the due date, he'd told her someone
else had bought it.

Sighing, she peered into her makeup mirror. *Grams would have loved Chris.* Picking
up her coral lipstick, she applied a fresh coat
to her lips. She fluffed the curls at the nape
of her neck and then lightly sprayed them
once more.

The doorbell rang. Glancing at the clock,
she knew it was Chris. Allowing Dylan or
Sondra to answer it so that she didn't seem
too anxious, she stood and walked in front
of the full-length mirror. Her gaze scanned
the simple, knee-length, aqua dress that
rested perfectly against her shape. The
spiked heels that she'd never before had the
courage to wear made her legs look long
and sleek, and she had to admit she'd never
felt so appealing.

A rush of heat flushed her cheeks. *I wish
Chris hadn't seen me in a face mask and curlers earlier.* She remembered his sweet words
just before he left. Looking in the mirror,
she whispered, "Well, I'm definitely not

wearing a potato sack." She twirled, allowing the hem of the dress to dance in the air. "I think he'll prefer this."

A soft knock sounded. "Chris is here," said Sondra. "Can I come in?"

"Yeah."

Sondra opened the door. She gasped. "Victoria, you look amazing!"

"Thank you."

"You better get out here before Chris paces a hole into my floor." She hooked her arm with Victoria's. "I've never seen him so nervous."

"That makes two of us."

Victoria walked down the hall and into the living room. Chris looked like the perfect gentleman in a navy blue suit and red silk tie. He looked up. Victoria sucked in her breath as his gaze scanned her briefly. "Hi, Chris. You look nice."

He nodded, and she watched his Adam's apple bop up and down. He stepped toward her. His height and breadth seemed to wrap around her. Touching her chin, he lifted her face until their gazes met. "You look amazing. You're absolutely beautiful, Vic."

She felt her cheeks warm at his sincere compliment and looked away to find Sondra and Dylan watching them. Sondra touched Dylan's arm and then dabbed her eyes as if she were Victoria's mother sending her daughter on her first date. Though much too close to Victoria's age, in a way Sondra had been a maternal figure for Victoria. She'd taught Victoria to cook, to clean, to care for herself. She glanced at PeeWee who had toddled into the room holding his sippy cup in one hand and a toy horse in the other. Sondra had also taught her how to care for others.

"We'd better get going. I'd say the chorus director would like for his chaperones to be on time." Chris touched her arm in a way that made her feel as though she belonged to him, as if he would protect her from anything that could ever happen. She loved the feeling.

"Okay." Allowing Chris to help her wrap her shawl around her shoulders, she then waved good-bye to her family and followed Chris to the front door.

"Close your eyes."

"What?" Victoria turned to find Chris mere inches from her cheek. His gaze seemed to grip hers, and she couldn't help noticing how easy it would be to lightly kiss his lips.

"I have a surprise." His breath raced against her ear, sending a shiver down her back. "Trust me. Just close your eyes."

Trust him. Trust him? She couldn't believe how much she trusted him. If he asked to drive her to an altar this night, she felt confident she would pledge her life to him. She closed her eyes, and he took her hand. The cool October air kissed her face and whipped through her hair. She gripped her shawl tighter with her free hand. Feeling the porch steps beneath her, she held tight to Chris's hand. Once the ground was beneath her feet, she asked, "Can I open them now?"

"Not yet." He stepped beside her, still holding her hand, only now his free hand touched the crook of her back. If only he would take her in his arms and declare his love for her. Surely Prince Charming would have claimed his princess by now, and she wanted so much to live happily ever after with Chris.

She listened as a car door opened. "Okay. You can look."

She opened her eyes. "Oh, Chris." Victoria covered her mouth with her hands. She gazed up at him and touched his arm. "It's Mary Ann."

"Yep." He smiled, and his eyes danced with merriment. "She's fixed. You don't have to worry about her anymore."

She slid inside the Corvette, inhaling the

scent of newly cleaned leather. Chris walked around and hopped inside. His frame barely fit inside the small car, but he beamed with excitement as he started the ignition. Buckling her seat belt, Victoria grinned. "I guess I didn't ruin her forever."

Chris gazed at her, his expression honest as a hard day's work. "You didn't ruin anything, my Mary Ann Mangler." He touched her hand, and a wave of pleasure wrapped around her. "You helped me restore a ruined relationship with my sister. That was worth every moment, every cent that went into repairing this old girl's bumper. If anything, I'd say I owe you."

"I'd say we're even. All those rides back and forth from town to the ranch. Getting to spend time with your sister. Feeling a part of a family." She felt her cheeks warm with the slip of the last statement. She looked at Chris, who simply smiled.

Once seated in the auditorium, Chris tapped the inside of his coat. Victoria's grandmother's ring was still nestled safe inside his pocket. He'd decided to follow his heart and ask Victoria to be his wife. Sure, he wanted to date her, but they'd spent so much time together over the last several months that he wanted to date her and plan their wedding at the same time.

He stared at her sitting beside him. The strands of curls that fell softly over her shoulders beckoned him. With every ounce of strength, he gripped the program and willed his fingers to keep to themselves. His gaze followed the slight curve of her jaw, tempting him to kiss his way to her lips.

He squelched a growl and looked away from her. *Besides, I'm not getting any younger.* He smiled as he thought of his twenty-seventh birthday in just a few weeks. In truth, he had plenty of time to date her, but he wanted any excuse he could conjure to make Victoria Thankful become Victoria *Ratliff.*

The concert ended, and a wisp of Victoria's perfume washed over him. He glanced over and found her leaning close. "I'm going to run to the ladies' room," she whispered.

Chris swallowed to keep from grabbing her, pulling her into his lap, and keeping her there for all time. He nodded and watched as she walked away.

"Abby is improving by leaps and bounds." A voice sounded from behind him.

Chris turned to find Mrs. Smith, Abby's music teacher, addressing him. "Yes, she is doing better."

"May I sit for a moment?" The older woman motioned toward Victoria's chair.

"Sure."

Mrs. Smith sat and clasped her hands in her lap. "I had been very worried about Abigail."

Chris bit back a chuckle. He hadn't heard anyone call her that in several years. In fact, the last time he recalled anyone calling her Abigail was when she'd sneaked a snake in the kitchen, nearly scaring their mother to death. Dad had come home and called for her using her full given name in order to come downstairs and receive her discipline.

"Since our father died and our mother left, I didn't know how to handle Abby. Victoria, the lady who's with me tonight, has done a world of good with her."

"Yes, since that lady crashed into your life" — the older woman snorted at her own joke — "she has made quite a difference for both of you. I noticed your car in the parking lot."

"Yep, she's all fixed up."

"That's good. I heard you took Abigail to buy her dress, as well." She smiled. "That was mighty brave of you. I've never been able to get my Bruce into a women's clothing store."

"Victoria made me see how much Abby

205

needed me. How she needed to feel a part of a family. That she had someone she could count on."

Mrs. Smith patted his hand. "You're a good man, Chris Ratliff, with a heart of gold. Any lady would be lucky to have you."

Chapter 18

"Any lady would be lucky to have you." Victoria snarled, mimicking the woman's words into her makeup mirror only moments after he had dropped her off after the concert. How dare Chris Ratliff pity her! His comments about her needing to feel part of a family echoed in her mind. She cringed at what she must have missed hearing him say when the waitress dropped and broke a plate beside her while Mrs. Smith and Chris were talking.

"How could I have been so foolish?" She took off her bracelet and placed it on the dresser. Victoria had actually believed she wanted to spend the rest of her life with that man. She snorted. *Yeah, here I've felt as though I've been on trial every day of my life for my daddy's mistakes, but I've always been honest. Mr. Ratliff, however, deserves an award for his ability to completely fool a crowd.* She gazed into her makeup mirror, watching as tears filled her eyes. "All this time, he's just been pitying me."

She thought of the kiss they'd shared in his truck. Goose bumps covered her skin, and she shivered. The connection she'd felt had been so real. Anger erupted inside her at her foolishness.

"What is it that scripture says?" She yanked off a high heel and threw it in the closet. "The heart is deceitful above all things." Pulling off the other, she tossed it in, as well. "And my heart has definitely deceived my mind. To think that I had even considered . . ." she fumed and turned away from the closet.

After taking off the pearl necklace, she slipped out of her dress and into her nightgown. She nestled into her sheets and pulled her Bible and prayer journal from the nightstand drawer. Not feeling completely ready to start her daily reading, she flipped through pages in her journal. Hardly a day had passed since she'd moved into the Wards' ranch that she didn't pray for Chris and Abby. They had become part of her family, in her heart at least.

"Why, God?" She glared at her ceiling. "Why was Chris just playing me? How could he have ever imagined that pretending to care for me would in any way make things better?"

A soft tap sounded on her door. "Vic?" Sondra's voice whispered.

"Yeah. Come on in."

The door opened, and Sondra handed her the phone. "You have a phone call."

"Who is it?"

"I don't know, but I'm going to put Emily to bed, so can you hang it up when you finish?"

"Sure." Victoria took the phone. Assuming it was Chris, she exhaled and braced herself for whatever lie he had to say. "Hello."

"Sugar!"

"Daddy?"

"I'm so glad you're there! Your mother and I just got home. My lawyer's about to prove me innocent. I'm going to be cleared."

"You're . . . what?"

"Yes, and I can hardly wait to see you. When can you come home?"

"But I thought . . ."

"You thought I was guilty, didn't you?"

"I guess I did." Victoria felt a sudden wave of guilt that she hadn't believed in her dad, followed by questions that pummeled her mind. "But you ran off."

"My lawyer's advice."

"And I had a wreck and no insurance."

"I just heard about that today. My policy was about to be renewed right before the charges were filed. Somehow it didn't get paid." He exhaled into the phone. "Oh, honey, I'm so sorry about that. I'm glad you're okay. We'll clear everything up when I get to see you. When can you come home?"

Victoria's mind raced. "I don't know." She thought of her chance to get her job back now that her dad was about to be found innocent. She thought of PeeWee and Emily. If she left, she didn't know when she'd see them again. And Abby. "Let me figure some stuff out, and I'll call you tomorrow."

"It's so good to hear your voice, sugar. I hated leaving like that." He exhaled again. "There's just so much to explain . . . in person." Her dad's tone was softer than she'd ever heard it. "And new things I want to share, as well."

"Yes, we do need to talk." Her heart burned with renewed feelings of the desertion she had experienced when she had awakened that morning several months before to find her parents gone.

A remembrance of trepidation washed over her and mixed with the twinge of excitement she felt at seeing her nephew and starting a new life on her own. Her head started to throb at the decisions she'd have to make, questions she needed answered. Her eyelid on one side began to twitch, a telltale sign of an oncoming stress migraine. She needed to go to bed, to not think for the moment. Chris . . . Abby . . . Daddy — it was too much. "I'll call you in the morning?"

"I love you."

Victoria was taken aback by her father's declaration. She hadn't heard those words from him in years. "I love you, too, Daddy."

She hung up the phone and looked down at her prayer journal. She'd come to the day when she'd read about how God has a time for everything. Closing her eyes, she begged God for guidance. Maybe the time had come for her to go home . . . to her parents. She could hear the tenderness in her father's voice. Maybe he had softened in other ways, as well. Maybe he would finally listen to her about his need for the Lord.

Her eyelid twitched more steadily, and heaviness rested on the top of her head. *I'm going to be sick if I don't go to sleep.*

She turned off the light, closed her eyes, and nestled into her covers. "God, it seems You've taken care of my life once again. The time has come for me to go home, to be a witness to Mother and Daddy."

■ ■ ■ ■

Chris took the box from his inside jacket pocket. He had planned to give Victoria the ring, but the evening just didn't seem to finish as he had hoped. When she'd returned from the restroom, Victoria seemed frustrated. She said something she ate must have disagreed with her, which he believed because his stomach had been in knots the whole night, as well.

"Didn't get to pop the question, huh, big brother?"

Chris turned to find Abby leaning against his bedroom door. She was a beautiful sight, all dressed up in her black gown with her hair all wrapped up on the top of her head and little curls hanging down all around. Makeup, no longer caked on her face, seemed to bring out the brightness in her eyes. Thanks to the patience and persistence and advice from Victoria, his little sister had grown up.

He shoved the box into his dresser drawer. "What are you talking about?"

Abby crossed her arms in front of her chest and grinned. "Come on, Chris. You are *way* too obvious. I knew you were getting ready to pop the question."

He smiled and leaned against the dresser. "Smart girl. You're right." He sighed and loosened his tie. "Didn't happen as I'd hoped."

"She'll say yes."

"You think so?"

Abby nodded. "Oh yeah. She loves you. She just doesn't fully realize it yet."

Chris took off his jacket. "I guess we'll have to wait and see." He turned back toward Abby. "But enough of that. How was your night?"

Abby giggled. "Wonderful. I think I really like Tyler."

"You do?"

"Yeah. He, like, pulled out my chair and everything. Really made me feel special." She shrugged. "I thought I liked Austin, but I don't know if he would have been as worried about me and what I was needing as Tyler was. In fact, did you see Austin?"

Chris shook his head. He wasn't sure if he'd seen anyone but Victoria tonight.

"He was flirting with Kelly the whole time Mallory was in the bathroom. I felt so bad for Mallory. I would have died if he'd done that to me. I'm glad he broke off our date."

Chris nodded. "Me, too."

Abby cocked her head and smiled. "I'm really glad we're friends again."

Chris walked over to her and wrapped her in a hug. "Me, too, little sis."

"How 'bout a game of Monopoly?" she mumbled into his chest.

Chris remembered the times he and Abby had set the game up on the dinner table and played for hours. He had always let her beat him.

"This time I'll beat you on my own," she added.

He released her. "What?"

"That's right." She smiled. "I knew you let me win, but I'm a big girl now. I'll whip you all by myself."

Chris chuckled. "You're on."

"Daddy, Mother, what are you doing here?" Victoria opened the front door wide.

Her father grabbed her in a hug and twirled her around. "I could hardly wait to get here." He put her back on her feet. "We just had to get up here to see our grandson."

"Grandson?"

Sondra walked up to them holding Pee-Wee on her hip. He buried his face in her cheek and clung to her neck. A slow, somewhat hesitant smile split her lips. "Hello, Thomas and Ethel. It's good to formally meet you."

Victoria raised her eyebrows and looked

from her sister-in-law to her parents. "Sondra, did you know they were coming?"

"We knew." Dylan's deep voice resounded from the hall. He walked toward them, holding Emily in one arm. He smiled and nodded his head toward her parents. "We're happy to have you in our home."

Victoria watched as her parents greeted Sondra and Dylan. Daddy seemed downright giddy to get to know them. He sneaked little tickles at PeeWee's sides and talked about cattle and ranching with Dylan. He even asked Sondra about her chick ministry. Mother proved much more hesitant. Polite. Proper. But hesitant. She held PeeWee for a moment, but when he started to play with the diamond pendant around her neck, she handed him back to Sondra.

"I can't believe you're here." Victoria took PeeWee in her arms when Sondra and Dylan announced they would get some refreshments for the family.

"Yes, well, it seems your father's had a change of heart these days," her mother murmured as she opened her purse and took out her compact.

Curiosity sped through Victoria's veins. Her father had changed. She could see it in his eyes, in his smile. It was in his countenance, in the way he spoke and carried

215

himself. *Oh, precious Jesus, could it be?*

"It seems your father has found the Lord." Her mother rolled her eyes and stared into her small mirror.

"Daddy?" Victoria gawked at her father, praying he would say what she hoped.

He smiled. "Your mother's right. I've found the Lord."

"Oh, Daddy!" Victoria stood and hugged her father again. "I'm so happy for you! How? When? What happened?"

He leaned forward in his chair. "When my lawyer called and said I needed to leave the country because I was being accused of embezzlement, I was stunned. I couldn't even move from my desk for several moments. My world was crumbling around me, and I could feel it. Every thought, every action I'd had in my life seemed to pass before me."

He clasped his hands. "All I could think about was his suggestion to leave you, my only living child. He said if I took you with me, people would believe you were guilty. I couldn't bear the thought of it.

"I'd already lost your brother." He stood and paced the floor. "How could I leave my baby girl, as well?" He stepped in front of her and touched a strand of her hair. "Then, for some reason, my childhood invaded my mind. Over and over again, I was in church with your grandma. The preacher's sermons about God's love, His grace, His mercy, His restoration kept running through my mind."

"Oh, Daddy." Victoria touched his hand.

He squeezed it tight. "When I got to the Cayman Islands, I sought out the first preacher I could find. Your mom thought I was nuts. . . ."

"Still think you're nuts," her mother murmured as she applied a fresh coat of lipstick to her mouth.

He chuckled. "But I had to know. Had to find out. Had to experience God's love. He showed me, honey. That preacher opened his Bible and showed me scriptures I'd long forgotten." Her daddy raked his fingers through his thinning hair and then swiped his hand over his tear-filled eyes.

"God was faithful and merciful to this old man. I got down on my knees and begged Jesus for forgiveness. I never embezzled money, but I sure did steal time from my wife, my son, and my little girl. And I lost all this time with my little grandson."

He nodded toward the kitchen. "I'm just thankful that Sondra and Dylan are willing to allow us to get to know him now."

Victoria wiped her own tear-filled eyes. She would have never imagined God would work things out so perfectly. "Daddy, I'm so happy, and I'm so glad you came."

"Me, too, sugar. And after we stay and visit a day or two, we'll all go home together."

Chris shut the door and kicked off his work boots. He'd been at the shop since before dawn, and the sun had descended into the ground some two hours before he made it home. He rubbed the back of his neck while he moved his head from side to side in an attempt to work out some of the crick that seemed to linger from the day before. The way he felt, he might have to bypass dinner and simply hit the sack.

"Chris, we have a guest." Abby's voice sounded quiet, winsome.

"A guest?" Chris walked into the kitchen and saw Abby holding Sassy-Girl close to her chest. An older, gray-haired woman sat across from her. With some difficulty, the woman placed her hand on the table and tried to stand.

"Please, you can sit." Chris walked over to her and offered his hand. "I'm Chris Ratliff. I don't think we've met."

She shook his hand. "I'm Junie Osborne. I'm glad to meet you."

"She was one of Mama's teachers when

she was a girl," said Abby.

Chris frowned. "I'm sorry, Ms. Osborne. We haven't seen our mother . . ."

"Mama was living with Ms. Osborne."

"What?" Chris fell into the chair beside the aged woman. "Where is Mama?"

The woman took off her oversized glasses and placed them on the table. A small tear traced her cheek. She wiped it away. "I'm so sorry. I had to come and tell you in person." She paused. "I'm afraid your mother has passed away."

Chris felt as if he'd been struck. He leaned back in his chair and swallowed the knot in his throat. He looked at Abby, who'd covered her face with a tissue. He pulled her, chair and all, over to him and wrapped his arms around her.

"You may not have known, but your mother had diabetes."

"We knew." Chris fought the eruption within him. Anger. Hurt. Sadness.

"About a year ago, Winnie showed up at my house. She was such a fragile thing, mourning her husband's death. I was happy to have her stay with me." The woman sighed. "I had a time getting your mother to take all her medication. I tried to convince her she'd feel better if she would take her depression medicine."

"Mama took medicine for depression?" Abby looked up at Chris.

"Yeah. Sometimes it's a symptom of diabetes, and Mama always struggled." Chris looked at Ms. Osborne. "Daddy used to have to coax her to take it. She'd feel better sometimes and wouldn't want it."

The woman nodded. "Yes, I'm sure that's true. Once I couldn't get her to take the depression medicine anymore, she gave up on eating right. Her diabetes was beginning to really affect her sight and her feet. She had another appointment to see my doctor the day . . ." The woman's voice caught. She stopped and took a tissue from her purse. "I'm sorry. I wanted so much to be strong for you, to make it easier to tell you."

"Go ahead." Chris held tightly to Abby. He'd allowed her to hurt alone once, but he wouldn't do it again.

"She slipped into a diabetic coma. The paramedics rushed her to the hospital, but she never woke from it." Ms. Osborne shook her head and touched Chris's hand. "I'm sorry I didn't contact you sooner. I didn't know . . ."

"She didn't tell you about us." *How could she? How could she care so little about us that in a year she never mentioned her own children?*

"She told me you were her relations. She had pictures of you all over her room. She kissed you good night every day. Without her medicine, she couldn't fight her depression."

"But how could she not tell you about us?" cried Abby.

"Listen, honey." Ms. Osborne leaned forward. "Your mama talked about you both constantly. She loved you. She just couldn't see clearly."

A knock sounded on the door. Chris stood.

"It's my cab."

"Your cab?" Chris looked at Ms. Osborne. She stood slowly and grabbed the cane that rested against the table.

"Here's my address." She handed Chris a slip of paper. "You come and get your mother's things whenever you and your sister are ready."

"Ma'am, you don't need a cab. I will be happy to take you —"

She touched his arm. "Stay with your sister. She needs you." Patting him, she added, "In the best way she knew how, your mother loved you both."

Chris nodded and helped her to the door. He watched as she and the driver walked to the cab and got inside. She was the only link he'd had to his mother in over a year. He'd never met the woman before, and she told him he'd never see his mother again.

"Deep down, I think I always knew Mama was depressed."

He nodded and allowed his heart to tender, to hurt, if for nothing else, for his sister. "Her diabetes was really bad, Abby."

"I know. But how could she not call us? How could she just up and die like that?" Abby cried. The finality of his mother's life began to sink into his heart. "Do you think she loved us?" whispered Abby.

Chris remembered Mama fixing cupcakes for them each year on their birthdays. He thought about how she always had one item that each member of the family liked for supper every single night. He remembered how she planted a specific flower for each of them in the garden each year. There were several things she did special for her family. "Yes, I think Ms. Osborne is right. She loved us."

Abby chuckled. "Remember how she used to sing 'Jesus Loves Me' at the top of her lungs in the shower?"

"I remember."

Abby wrapped her arms around his waist. "Mama had a beautiful voice."

"Yes, she did."

"I'm going to miss her." She tightened her hold. "But at least we know where she is."

Chris exhaled. *Thank You, God, for telling us. Now we can heal, and Mama has been made whole with You.* "Yes, we do."

CHAPTER 19

Victoria pulled her Suburban into the street parking space. She grabbed her purse and the picnic basket and walked toward Lawton's community park. The warmer-than-usual November air whipped through her hair. Despite the higher temperature, Victoria could feel the oncoming of cooler weather. The leaves, a mixture of red and golden hues, were also proof of it.

Three days had passed since the chorus concert, and she hadn't spoken to Chris. She had decided to go home with her parents the following day. Dylan, Sondra, and even Zack had tried to talk her into staying, but she knew she couldn't. Her heart belonged to Chris, and she had to get over him.

Abby. She dreaded telling her young friend of her plan to leave. Victoria's love for Abby was every bit as strong as if the girl had been born into her own family. Hoping Chris would still be at the shop, Victoria planned to drive by their house and talk to Abby before going back to the ranch. *God, You'll have to walk me through that conversation.*

Shaking her head, she determined to ponder that later in the day. For now, she needed to find Zack. Peering around the park, she spied him already sitting on the bench with his script and a cooler of drinks. He waved, and she picked up her pace.

She had been surprised at what a wonderful actor and singer Zack proved to be. He had really taken the community play seriously, and she had a feeling, come this weekend when he was able to try out, that Zack would have the lead male part in Lawton's version of *Oklahoma*.

"Hi, Zack." She lifted the picnic basket a little higher. "Do you want to eat first or practice first?"

"I'm starving. How 'bout we eat first?"

She opened the basket and pulled out some paper plates and napkins. "Sounds like a plan to me. I brought homemade chicken salad sandwiches, compliments of Sondra, a bag of chips, carrot sticks, and some yummy brownies, made especially for us by PeeWee and yours truly."

"Mmm. Delicious. And I brought some drinks." He opened the cooler. "I think I got the easy end of this deal."

"Don't you worry about that. PeeWee and I had a blast putting this basket together. Emily even joined in and threw a few carrot sticks at us."

Zack sobered. "It's going to be hard to leave them, huh?"

"Unbelievably. I don't know how I will do it." Victoria placed the sandwiches on the plates and then opened the bag of chips. She grabbed one and popped it into her mouth, willing herself not to envision driving away from her new family. "My parents and I are leaving tomorrow. I've already packed."

"I haven't heard anything about your dad's case on the TV."

"It's not been finalized in court. But soon."

"It all happened so fast. Their coming back. Your dad's change of heart. Your leaving."

Fast didn't even begin to describe it. Victoria felt as if she'd been caught up in a whirlwind. She'd been praying for God's guidance, but everything seemed to be coming at her quicker than she could be sure of His answers.

"I know. I could hardly believe it. And he and Mother are finally getting the chance to meet their grandson. Once they saw Pee-Wee, they couldn't deny he was Kenny's." She bit into her sandwich and then took a drink. "And Dylan has been amazing about letting them stay. He's a truly wonderful man." She smacked her leg. "But enough about me. How is Rosa?"

He smiled. "Beautiful."

Victoria giggled. "Have you talked to her yet?"

"No."

"When do you plan on it?"

"I don't know that I'll ever get up the nerve."

"Sure you will. Tryouts are this weekend. Talk to her then."

Zack dipped his head and played with his napkin. "I'll try."

"You'd better, because I'm coming back for the play, and you'd better be dating Rosa by then."

Zack smiled again. "I hope so."

Victoria stood up. "Ya ready to practice?"

"Ready as ever."

Chris splashed some cologne on his chest. It had been three full days since he'd seen or talked to Victoria. Every vehicle in Lawton had decided to break down in some form or fashion. He'd been working sixteen-hour days, but all he could think of was when he could see her again.

He grabbed his tie and put it around his neck. He'd called the ranch to see if Victoria would spend the day with him. Sondra had told him she'd gone to the park to rehearse for Lawton's community play. *I didn't even know Victoria acted.* There was still so much to learn about each other, and he longed to spend every single day of the rest of his life learning every facet of Victoria Thankful's personality.

Opening his dresser drawer, he picked up the small black box tucked away inside. He popped the top and gazed at the small ring. Knowing it had meant so much to Victoria, he couldn't wait to see her face when he presented it to her. He shut it and placed it in his pants pocket. Sliding into his coat jacket, he grabbed his keys.

"Today's the day?"

Chris peered back at his sister. "Yep."

She walked over to him and adjusted his tie. "You look very nice."

"Thanks."

"I can't wait to have a big sister."

Chris smiled. "I can't wait for you to have one either." He leaned down and kissed Abby on the cheek and then walked out the door.

The park will be a beautiful place to propose, and it's such a nice day. He stopped at the florist's shop and picked up a dozen red roses. He envisioned her sitting on the park bench reading the lines of the play. Her long hair whipping in the wind. He could almost smell her sweet scent and feel the softness of her cheek. He would take her hand in his, get down on one knee, and declare his love for her.

Turning onto the park's street, he saw her Suburban, and his heart raced. He experienced a mixture of excitement and nerves. Pulling Mary Ann into the space behind her vehicle, he closed his eyes and offered a quick prayer to the Lord for courage. As he reached for the roses, he realized his hands had grown clammy, so he wiped them on his pants legs. Exhaling a slow breath to calm his nerves, he grabbed the flowers and opened the door.

A smile split his lips as a song of praise filled his mind. He'd never been so excited, so sure of a decision in his life. He could hardly wait to make her his wife, to take her into his arms, to kiss her as a man kisses his wife. With purpose, he walked into the park.

He saw her.

He gasped.

Zack Bradshaw knelt before her. He held

one of her hands in his.

Chris's heart dropped as Victoria nodded.

CHAPTER 20

Disillusioned, Chris turned away. *I don't think they saw me.* He couldn't bear the thought of speaking to either one of them. How could he have been so wrong, so stupid? He didn't even know Zack and Victoria had spent any real time together. *Well, she had hugged him at church, agreeing to meet him somewhere.*

His heart thudded against his chest. Then why had she gone with him to the chorus dinner? To appease Abby, he supposed. But why had she kissed him in his truck? Why? *God, I love her. I was so sure she was the right one for me.*

A sudden fury filled his gut as he envisioned Zack holding Victoria in his arms. He couldn't bear the thought of it. He wouldn't bear the thought of it. He loved Victoria, and he was willing to fight for her. Turning on his heels, he bounded back up the sidewalk toward the woman he had every intention of spending the rest of his life with. "Victoria," he called.

She turned toward him. "Chris?"

Chris closed the last few steps between them, threw the roses to the ground, and took her hands into his. He looked at Zack. "I like you, Zack, but I have to do this." He gazed back at Victoria. "I can't stand by and let this happen. You cannot marry Zack." He pointed to his chest. "I love you. I want you to be my wife."

"What?"

"And I won't take no for an answer. I don't know what has happened here. I didn't even know you and Zack were spending time together, but I'm willing to do whatever I need to, to show you that I am the right man for you."

Zack started to laugh. Chris glared at him. "This is not funny."

He covered his mouth and hunkered down. "I'm sorry," he mumbled. Grabbing the cooler, he added, "I think I'll leave now."

Chris snorted and peered back at Victoria. "See there. The slightest bit of opposition comes his way, and Zack is hitting the high road."

Victoria crossed her arms in front of her chest and stomped her foot. "You are making no sense. What are you talking about,

Chris Ratliff?"

He grabbed her arms. "I'm saying I won't let you marry Zack. I love you. I want you to be my wife."

Victoria frowned. "Why would you think I'm marrying Zack? I'm not marrying Zack. We're friends."

"But . . ." Chris released her arms. "But he just asked you to marry him, and you nodded yes."

Victoria shook her head. "No, he didn't."

"Yes, he did. I saw it."

Victoria's mouth opened in a perfect O, and she covered her lips with her hand. A small giggle escaped. "We were practicing the play."

"The play?"

"The community play. Zack is trying out and asked me to help with his lines."

"I thought you were trying out."

Victoria shook her head. "No, I was helping him. Where would you ever get the notion that I was trying out?"

Heat raced up Chris's spine into his neck and to his cheeks. "So you didn't just accept a proposal from Zack?"

"Nope. In fact, Zack's got a bit of a crush on Rosa from church."

"He does?"

She nodded.

"I guess I've made a big ol' fool of myself then."

Victoria nodded again, and Chris bent down and picked up the roses. He tried to straighten them out a bit and then extended them toward Victoria. "Can I try again?"

Sighing, Victoria stepped away from him. "I don't want your pity, Chris."

"My pity?"

"Yes. I heard what you said to Abby's teacher."

He scratched his head. "Now *I* don't have a clue what *you* are talking about."

"I heard you the night of the chorus dinner." She crossed her arms in front of her chest. "I heard you say that I just needed to feel a part of a family." She opened her arms wide. "Well, you know what, Chris Ratliff? I did feel a part of your family. I wanted to be a part of your family, but not out of pity." She turned away from him. "Never out of pity."

Chris tried to recall what Victoria was talking about. Then he remembered Mrs. Smith talking to him about Abby. He smiled and touched Victoria's arm. She flinched. "Vic, I wasn't talking about you. Mrs. Smith and I were talking about Abby. I said that Abby needed to feel a part of a family." He walked around her so that he could face her.

"I told her you had made us like a family again."

Victoria peeked up at him. "You did?"

He nodded and touched her cheek. "I think we're both a little goofy." He caressed her skin with his thumb. "Victoria, I love you."

"Promise?"

The sincerity, the sweet honesty that shone through her eyes never ceased to nearly unravel him. He could read her wants and her desires so perfectly in her gaze. "Oh, Vic." He ran the back of his hand down her cheek and jaw. When she closed her eyes, he traced her lips with his index finger. "I promise."

She opened her eyes and wrapped her arms around him. She kissed his lips quickly. "Oh, Chris, I love you, too. I've been miserable these last few days. So much has happened that I want to share with you."

"I've been so busy, and I have so much to tell, as well." He stuck his hand in his pocket and pulled out the black box. Getting on one knee, he took her hand in his. "But I want to spend every day of the rest of my life hearing everything you want to share with me."

He opened the box, and Victoria gasped and placed her hand on her chest. "My grandma's ring. I thought it was gone forever."

"I made a deal with the pawnshop owner. If you weren't able to purchase it before the time was up, I'd buy it. I did, and I hoped, knowing how much it meant to you, that you would want to wear it as my wife."

Joy surged through her as if she'd been struck by lightning. "I had always hoped to wear it. Oh, Chris." She jumped into his lap, almost knocking him to the ground. "Of course I'll marry you."

Victoria took a quick bite of the cream cheese–covered bagel Sondra had brought from the ranch. If she didn't stop eating, she'd never be able to squeeze into the bodice-fitted dress she and her mother had picked out. "I think I'm weird."

Sondra furrowed her eyebrows. "Weird?"

Victoria nodded. "How many brides do you know who can't *stop* eating on their wedding day?"

Sondra laughed and rubbed her blossoming belly. "Weirder things have happened. Try having three kids in a little over three years!"

Emily toddled toward her mother and wrapped her arms around Sondra's leg. Her little bit of light brown hair had been coaxed up into the tiniest ponytail Victoria had ever seen. Victoria bent down and tightened the satin bow at Emily's tummy. "You look like a little princess."

"Well, what do you think, sis?"

Victoria turned at the sound of Abby's voice behind her. She gasped and stood to her full height. Drinking in her soon-to-be sister-in-law's long, dark curls swooped up and away from her face but down her back, Victoria could hardly believe the perfect fit of the light green satin gown that streamed down her shape. "You're the most beautiful maid of honor I've ever seen."

"I agree." Ethel tousled a few of Abby's curls.

Victoria bit back the spilling of emotion that threatened at the tenderness between her mother and Abby. Though her mother hadn't made a commitment to Christ yet, the embezzlement scare had frightened her enough that she was valuing her time with Victoria as well as taking Abby under her wing as a second daughter. Victoria was sure it was just a matter of time before her mother also recognized her own need for a Savior.

"Lizzie's ready, as well." Grace walked into their makeshift dressing room that was actually one of the Sunday school classes.

She placed her hand in the small of her back and stretched. "I wouldn't mind if this baby decided to come right this minute." Her cell phone started to ring. Pulling it out of her purse, she looked at the caller ID and shook her head. "Eric Nichols is the biggest mother hen I know. I better get on out there before he comes looking for me."

Emily released her mom and ran for Lizzie. She grabbed the older girl's hand and swung it back and forth. Victoria smiled. "You two are the prettiest flower girls ever."

"Definitely. Now I think we'd better be getting you into your dress," said Ethel.

Abby agreed. "Yep. My brother will be beating down this door if you're not down at that altar when you're supposed to be."

Victoria bit back a chuckle, as she believed Abby to be exactly right. Slipping into her dress, she inhaled, wishing she'd eaten one less bagel as her mom fastened each clasp. With a final once-over, her mother hugged her and then left to go to her place at the back of the church to await one of the ushers to escort her to her seat.

"You ready?" Her daddy's voice sounded from outside the door.

"Yes." She opened it and watched as her father's eyes glazed.

"Oh, honey, you're beautiful."

Victoria felt her own eyes mist, and she swatted her hands in front of her face. "Daddy, don't make me cry. My makeup will smear, and my freckles will pop out."

He placed her hand into the crook of his arm. "Your freckles are beautiful."

She allowed him to guide her to the back of the church. She tried to see Chris through the crack of the door but couldn't. Instead she sneaked peeks of Abby, Sondra, Lizzie, and Emily as they started their descents down the aisle. Finally, it was her turn. The doors were opened wide, and she saw the altar . . . and Chris!

His eyes widened, and a smile split his lips. Her heart fluttered, and even from a distance, he made her feel as if she were the most special woman in the world. The aisle seemed too long. Her dad moved too slowly. She wanted to be beside the man she loved. She could hardly wait to say her vows and have Chris take her into his arms as his one and only.

"Aunt Vic's pretty."

Her sweet nephew's voice echoed through the church. Among the laughter, Victoria skimmed the crowd and saw Zack and Rosa holding hands in a middle row. She grinned and then gazed at PeeWee. He stood tall and proud beside the only daddy he'd ever known.

His face lit up with pure happiness, and Victoria had never been so thankful that God had allowed a tragedy to be the biggest blessing He had ever bestowed. Not only had she become a part of a family in Lasso but one with her own parents, as well.

Closing the distance between them, Chris took her hand in his. The coarseness of his palm scratched hers, and she relished the feel of it. Her man worked hard, completely, and with integrity. He loved the same way.

She gazed up at him and noted her burly fellow's eyes glistened with the threat of tears. He leaned over and whispered, "You're beautiful, my Mary Ann Mangler."

She smiled. "I love you."

"I love you." His gaze spoke of his commitment and yearning.

They turned and faced the pastor. *There is a time for everything,* God's Word spoke to her heart, *and a season for every activity. . . .* Victoria thought of all the seasons of life she'd weathered this year — the alleged embezzlement, the wreck, her first job, Pee-Wee, Abby . . . and Chris. *Maybe God will use me to help.* Chris's words from the night of their first kiss ran through her mind.

And He had. Chris had shown her patience when precious treasures were damaged, he'd shown her strength when people in their lives were tough, and he'd shown her love, even when he thought it wouldn't be returned. God had used Chris, and Victoria longed to see what God would show them for the rest of their lives together.

They turned to face each other to recite their vows. Chris leaned over and whispered, "I've never felt so blessed."

Victoria gazed up at him. "By His hand . . . neither have I."

ABOUT THE AUTHOR

Jennifer Johnson and her unbelievably supportive husband, Albert, are happily married and raising Brooke, Hayley, and Allie, the tree cutest young ladies on the planet. Besides being a middle school teacher, Jennifer loves to read, write, and chauffeur her girls. She is a member of American Christian Fiction Writers. Blessed beyond measure, Jennifer hopes to always think like a child — bigger than imaginable and with complete faith. Send her a note at jenwrites4god@bellsouth.net.

The employees of Thorndike Press hope you have enjoyed this Large Print book. All our Thorndike and Wheeler Large Print titles are designed for easy reading, and all our books are made to last. Other Thorndike Press Large Print books are available at your library, through selected bookstores, or directly from us.

For information about titles, please call:
(800) 223-1244

or visit our Web site at:
http://gale.cengage.com/thorndike

To share your comments, please write:
Publisher
Thorndike Press
295 Kennedy Memorial Drive
Waterville, ME 04901